**"I've been thinking about you."**

"You don't have to lie to me, O'Hare," Kinga said. "I know exactly what that night was."

"And what was it, Kinga?" Griff asked her.

"A wild night, a step out of time, something that wouldn't be repeated."

"It was wild, it was unexpected. It's also a night that I can't stop thinking about. I can't stop thinking about *you*."

Yeah, she didn't believe that for one second.

"You don't believe me. Look, I didn't call you because I was out of town. I had...something to take care of."

"Griff, it's fine. I didn't expect you to call, won't expect you to call and understand that this is, apart from one night, a completely professional relationship."

"Except that I want another night and, possibly, another night after that."

"Sorry?"

"I'd very much like to share your bed again, Kinga. Any chance of that happening?"

\* \* \*

*Secrets of a Bad Reputation* by Joss Wood
is part of the Dynasties: DNA Dilemma series.

Dear Reader,

Welcome to the luxurious world of the Ryder-Whites!

Callum Ryder-White is the most talented businessman of his generation—a "problem patriarch" who pushes his family to be the very best...and then constantly undermines them. Callum's Christmas gift to each member of his family, a DNA ancestry test, sets off a chain of unexpected events for the Ryder clan.

Kinga is organizing the famous Ryder International Ball and Callum wants Griff O'Hare—a gorgeous, famous musician with an awful reputation—to perform. She has enough to deal with due to a controlling grandfather and a stressful career. She doesn't need to be attracted to a bad boy like Griff. But what if his past behavior is all a lie and her bad boy is actually a good guy?

Happy reading!

*Joss*

xxx

Connect with me on:

Facebook: JossWoodAuthor
Twitter: JossWoodbooks
BookBub: joss-wood
www.JossWoodBooks.com

# JOSS WOOD

——

## SECRETS OF A BAD REPUTATION

HARLEQUIN

## DESIRE

# HARLEQUIN®
## DESIRE™

ISBN-13: 978-1-335-73547-8

Secrets of a Bad Reputation

Copyright © 2022 by Joss Wood

This edition published by arrangement with Harlequin Books S.A.

For questions and comments about the quality of this book,
please contact us at CustomerService@Harlequin.com.

Harlequin Enterprises ULC
22 Adelaide St. West, 41st Floor
Toronto, Ontario M5H 4E3, Canada
www.Harlequin.com

**Printed in U.S.A.**

**Joss Wood** loves books, coffee and traveling—especially to the wild places of southern Africa and, well, anywhere. She's a wife and a mom to two young adults. She's also a slave to two cats and a dog the size of a small cow. After a career in local economic development and business, Joss writes full-time from her home in KwaZulu-Natal, South Africa.

### Books by Joss Wood

### Harlequin Desire

#### *Dynasties: DNA Dilemma*

*Secrets of a Bad Reputation*

#### *Murphy International*

*One Little Indiscretion*
*Temptation at His Door*
*Back in His Ex's Bed*

### Harlequin Presents

#### *South Africa's Scandalous Billionaires*

*How to Undo the Proud Billionaire*
*How to Win the Wild Billionaire*

Visit her Author Profile page at Harlequin.com, or josswoodbooks.com, for more titles.

You can also find Joss Wood on Facebook, along with other Harlequin Desire authors, at Facebook.com/harlequindesireauthors!

# Prologue

*James*
*Christmas Day*

James Ryder-White carefully folded the classy gold paper and placed it on his knee, mentally rolling his eyes at the square, red velvet box it revealed. An other Christmas, another pair of designer cuff links from Penelope...

His wife was not the most original present giver in the world. Then again, he'd gifted her with a black cashmere sweater and another solid gold charm to add to her already heavy bracelet. James knew she was as enthusiastic about his gift as he was about hers.

They'd been married too long, knew each other

too well, and neither of them made an effort anymore. If they ever had.

James looked out the window of his childhood home—he and Pen occupied the right wing of his father's enormous mansion—and sighed at the wet sleet slapping the floor-to-ceiling windows. He loved Portland, Maine, with its arty vibe and excellent food scene, its centuries-old lighthouses, historic homes and edgy, independent shops and boutiques.

But this particular piece of craggy coastline was home. Low clouds obscured the jaw-dropping views of Dead Man's Cove. Ryder's Rest, his father's estate fourteen miles north of Portland, on Cousin's Island, consisted of a seven-bedroom mansion—every room in the house had a view of the bay—with heated pools, multiple decks and patios, and a garage big enough for ten automobiles.

It also boasted a drive-on stone pier and dock, three deepwater moorings, and over eight hundred feet of beach frontage.

James loved this house and property. The owner? Not so much.

He leaned back in his chair and briefly closed his eyes, wondering what his life would've been like had he not married Pen thirty-some years ago.

What if he'd had the guts to defy his father, to take a chance, to forge his own path? James ran a hand over his face, pushing his what-if thoughts away. He'd witnessed his father's ruthlessness—toward business rivals and members of his own family—so defying Callum had never been an option.

James also liked the money and the status of being a Ryder-White, so he remained a good little soldier. His obedience resulted in plump pockets and fat bank accounts. Putting up with Callum's crap allowed James to buy property and flashy cars and establish trust funds for his children.

His daughters now controlled the money he'd gifted them, and Kinga's and Tinsley's fortunes were still, as far as he knew, intact.

Kinga, brown-eyed and blonde, sat down on the arm of his chair, interrupting his musings. James placed a hand on her back, grateful for the connection. Whenever regrets slapped him hot and hard, he reminded himself that if not for Pen, he wouldn't have two smart, lovely daughters. His marriage was far from a love match, but his two girls made any sacrifices worthwhile.

"Daddy, you're looking a little melancholy this lovely Christmas morning."

"I'm fine, Mouse."

And James supposed that he was. His marriage functioned, his children were healthy and successful. He wished he could add happy to that list, but Kinga was plagued by a life-changing event that had happened a decade ago and Tinsley was taking a long time to come to terms with her divorce.

Happiness: such a vague concept, and as hard to capture as the morning mist.

James felt Kinga straighten and he raised his head, softly sighing when he noticed his father—sharp blue eyes in a craggy face—standing by the fireplace, impatiently waiting for his family to pay attention. Callum was close to eighty, but he was fit and healthy, mentally and physically.

Callum caught James's eye and angled his head. James cleared his throat, and Tinsley and Penelope immediately stopped talking, their eyes wary. James understood the emotion—Callum had a habit of dropping new ideas—or orders—on the family whenever they gathered socially.

It wouldn't matter to Callum that it was Christmas; the Ryder-White reputation and businesses were always his highest priorities. Actually, James was surprised Callum had waited this long to raise Ryder International business.

"You will have noticed that I failed to give you all a gift this year," he said, his deep voice and cold blue eyes commanding attention.

Callum linked his hands behind his back, his nose in the air. Oh, God, here came the lecture. How many times had he heard it? A hundred times? Two hundred? More?

Probably.

"As you know, the first Ryder was William Ryder who arrived in Maine during the third settlement of this area. He was one of the original owners of property. He married the wealthy Lottie White, and we are directly descended from them. I've been reading up on genealogy and I want a deeper understanding of our family roots."

This. *Again*. The family tree stretched back three hundred years and their unbroken bloodline was a badge Callum wore with pride. But really, how much more was there to discover?

"Apparently, it is now possible to pinpoint where, geographically, our ancestors resided, and I want to know," Callum continued. "None of you have expressed an interest in our lineage and I am greatly disappointed in you all. To encourage that interest, my Christmas gift to you is a DNA test, so you can have a better understanding of your heritage."

James watched his father pull test tubes from a brown envelope and took the tube Callum handed him.

"Just swipe the swab on the inside of your mouth and put it back into the tube. Write your name on the label." Callum barked instructions, handing tubes to Pen and Kinga and Tinsley.

"I registered us on WhoAreYou.com." Callum spun the top of his test tube and pulled out a long Q-tip. "I will send off our DNA next week and soon we will have a complete picture of our origins."

"Technology is amazing," Callum added after he'd finished swabbing the inside of his mouth, sounding pleased. "WhoAreYou is the biggest and most popular company providing this service. I have distant cousins that are already registered on the site, so the site should throw up a match to them. I have asked to be notified if there are any DNA matches to me or any of you. It's a very good way to fill in some blanks on the family tree."

James felt the room swim. He stared at the test tube, his mind racing. How could he get out of this?

"This isn't difficult," Callum snapped, looking from him to Penelope, who held her test tube in her hand. "What's the problem?"

"No problem, Callum," James lied. He'd never been allowed to call him father. Or Dad.

James looked at his wife, noticing the annoyance in her eyes. She squirmed in her chair, and sent Callum a narrowed-eyed, I'm-not-happy look.

Callum replaced the swabbed-with-saliva tubes in the envelope. "Let's discuss business."

Blood and business, that was all that was important to Callum. "Have you made any progress tracking down the owner of that block of shares, James?"

James ground his back teeth together. Over the past three decades, Callum's obsession with the 25 percent stake in Ryder International he didn't control had mushroomed and he was more determined than ever to buy the shares back. But first they needed to discover who owned them.

"I'm still working on it."

"Work harder," Callum snapped. "Let's talk about Ryder International's centennial celebrations. The charity ball will kick off the year-long celebration," Callum continued. The ball was a $100,000-a-plate function, limited to two thousand very rich, very exclusive people, including princes and politicians. "I thought you girls would've nailed down a performer by now."

Kinga and Tinsley ran Ryder's enormous PR division together and did an excellent job. Their talent was something Callum routinely overlooked and rarely acknowledged.

"The performer I booked has canceled all her performances for the next six months for medical reasons," Kinga replied. "I'm still looking for someone."

"Well, I want someone a little controversial, someone who will attract attention and—what's that word?—*buzz*."

James felt Kinga stiffen. "And do you have any suggestions as to who might provide that for us?" she asked, her eyebrows raised.

"Griff O'Hare."

Kinga exchanged horrified glances with Tinsley and James didn't blame them. Even he'd heard of the bad boy singer, performer and actor with the voice of an angel and the impulse control of a toddler.

Kinga just closed her eyes and shook her head. "Happy damn Christmas to me."

# One

Sitting in a booth in Ryder International's flagship bar situated in the famous Forrester-Grantham Hotel in Manhattan, Kinga Ryder-White tapped an impatient finger against her glass and scowled at the face of her Piaget watch.

Griff O'Hare was extremely late for their meeting but that didn't surprise her. She wouldn't hold her breath waiting for him.

Honestly, what was Callum thinking wanting someone so disreputable as the headline act at one of the most highly anticipated social events of the decade? Nothing good ever came of her irascible grandfather meddling in PR affairs.

Yesterday, when she was summoned to Callum's office, he'd gestured Kinga to look at his massive flat-screen TV. Her grandfather was watching You-Tube, a surprise in itself. Her scowl deepened when she saw Griff O'Hare in the video—wearing holey-at-the-knees jeans and a red T-shirt—sitting at a piano in a music studio.

She couldn't deny that he was talented. And hot.

"I don't want to hire him, Callum."

Callum ignored her, pushed Play, and O'Hare's rich voice filled Callum's office, deep and dark and magical. She recognized the song and was marginally impressed that the bad boy of rock and roll could control himself long enough to give a creditable rendition of "Nessun Dorma."

When the video finished, Kinga had turned to Callum and shrugged. "I never said he couldn't sing. I said he isn't someone I want performing at the ball."

"I will make that call, not you," Callum had retorted, throwing the remote onto his desk.

Yes, *of course*. Because, in Callum's world, a woman couldn't possibly make a decision without having a male approve it. Kinga controlled her urge to scream. She and Callum had a hate-hate relationship: he hated her sassy mouth and lack of deference, and she hated the way he treated her father and his frequent dismissal of her and Tinsley's opinions.

She loved her job, loved the people she worked with…but couldn't stand her boss.

Callum had nodded to the screen. "That video has had over sixty-five million views in a month. The music world is speculating on when he'll return to performing."

She'd stared at the view count, her eyes skimming the comments. Ah, this was starting to make sense now. Griff O'Hare was unreliable, but he was a superbly talented, currently elusive rock star, and the world was clamoring for his return.

Callum Ryder-White wanted to be the person credited for bringing O'Hare back into the limelight by having his first performance in, well, *forever* be at the Ryder International ball. Callum always wanted everything and anything that was new, shiny, exclusive and expensive.

He was, after all, the patriarch of the Ryder-White family, and he considered himself to be East Coast royalty. And kings wanted what they wanted…

*Blergh.*

Nope, hiring the unreliable O'Hare was far too risky. Kinga shook her head. "I'm not comfortable with his return performance being at my ball."

"*My* ball," Callum had corrected her. "My company, my ball, my decision. Meet with him, and make it happen. Or else find a new job. Now go away."

Kinga, knowing it was useless to argue, had left. But she couldn't help wondering if her grandfather was serious or if he was playing her, setting her up for failure. Callum did like to play manipulative mind games. Whatever he was up to, Kinga had no intention of risking *her* carefully planned event being spoiled when the entertainment failed to show.

Since that meeting with Callum she'd done her homework, conducted research on the guy and concluded that Griff O'Hare—once voted the world's sexiest man—was an ass.

Even worse, he was a bad boy ass.

Kinga had no time for either—bad boys or asses.

Kinga scowled, decided she'd give him another thirty minutes and then she'd move on. She didn't have time to waste on tardy one-time superstars who thought they were God's gift.

She liked New York City but she didn't love it; Portland—her proud little city, smaller, cleaner and far lovelier—was home. And she needed to get back.

On the point of leaving, she felt the atmosphere in the bar change, heard the buzz of excited voices and assumed her four-thirty appointment had deigned to join her. Lifting her head, she watched Griff O'Hare flash his famous half smile, half smirk at the excited waitress. Most of the men drinking in the luxury bar wore designer suits and thousand-dollar shoes—hair neatly brushed, ties precisely knotted and beards carefully trimmed—but O'Hare flouted the dress code with his faded jeans ripped at the knee, biker boots and a leather bomber jacket, a matte black helmet tucked under his arm. His nut-brown, naturally shot-with-gold hair was overlong and messy, and a thick layer of stubble covered his strong jaw.

A vibe of I-don't-give-a-crap rolled off him.

If she were honest, she'd admit her stomach did feel a bit mushy, her skin prickly. But that was just biology. She, like most women, was programmed by evolution to look for the fittest, strongest, most masculine guy in the room as a potential mate.

But Kinga, relentlessly single, needed more than an attractive face topping a ripped body. There were other, more important traits she required in a partner. Fidelity, a solid work ethic, intelligence.

But none of that mattered, since she no longer believed in love, didn't know if she ever had. But even if she did, and had, she'd never again risk losing a person she loved.

She knew how that felt and it wasn't an experience she needed to repeat.

O'Hare handed his helmet and his jacket to the simpering waitress and Kinga noticed how his navy blue T-shirt skimmed a wide chest and how the bands of the sleeves were tight against his big biceps.

With his seductive swagger and easy confidence, he screamed trouble.

Her ball was luxurious, classy, upmarket and elegant; she needed a performer who reflected those qualities. O'Hare would not fill the bill. She just had to get through this meeting and bring Callum around to her way of thinking. She'd find someone else.

O'Hare looked around, saw her sitting in the booth, and their eyes collided. Heat skittered up her spine and lodged in her womb, warming the space between her legs. Her nipples contracted and she swallowed a heavy sigh.

Sue her, she was attracted. But only on a purely physical level.

Kinga watched as he looked around the bar for

someone to stand and approach him. Deciding that it wouldn't hurt him to be kept waiting for a few minutes, she leaned against the back of the leather-clad booth, curious to see what he'd do. He looked around again and Kinga saw the flash of irritation at having his time wasted.

*Welcome to my world, dude.*

Enjoying herself, Kinga kept her eyes on him. When their gazes clashed again, Kinga felt the same slap of attraction. Damn, this was neither helpful nor convenient.

O'Hare lifted those swimmer's shoulders in a what-the-hell shrug and her stomach tightened as he moved toward her, his eyes not leaving her face. Stopping at her booth, he jammed his hands into the front pockets of his jeans, and Kinga inhaled his fresh air and healthy male scent and felt her head swim.

*Keep it together, Ryder-White. He's just another guy and this is just another meeting.*

That was like saying Hurricane Sandy was just another storm.

"Well, huh."

Kinga raised one eyebrow. "Sorry?"

"Your eyes are the color of fine, old whiskey."

"And have been since I was born," Kinga pertly replied, telling herself not to blush. *Business meeting, Kinga! Be professional.*

He sent her a slow, hot, sexy smile and her stomach did a full, twisting forward tuck, something she'd never mastered in five years of gymnastic training.

"I'm looking for a business associate but if I don't find him, can I buy you a drink?"

He flashed her a smile and looked a little confused when she leaned back against the leather banquette and raised an unimpressed eyebrow.

After thirty seconds of silence, Kinga nodded to the seat opposite her and narrowed her eyes. "No, O'Hare, you can't *buy me a drink*. But feel free to sit down. I'm Kinga Ryder-White and you are disrespectfully late."

Well, *shit*. Kinga Ryder-White looked like she'd swallowed a particularly sour lemon.

Not the reaction he generally received, Griff thought, a little amused. Having been a so-called heartthrob since his early teens, he found her get-over-yourself attitude refreshing.

Griff slid into the booth, his eyes sliding down her face and elegant neck. He leaned sideways to peek at the rest of her long, lean body. She was tall for a woman, five-eight or five-nine, but, topping out at six-four, he'd guess he still had four or five inches on her.

She was dressed in what he called Boring Corporate, a men's style button-down shirt, black tailored pants and spiky-heeled boots. Her makeup, if she wore any, was minimal and made her skin look flawless. Griff had dated enough women to know that natural look took hours to perfect.

Then those astute, exceptional eyes met his and he realized he wasn't dealing with a naive young woman or a pushover. She was not only sexy but also smart, determined and very, very wary.

"I thought I was meeting with Callum Ryder-White," he said, raking his hand through his hair.

"My grandfather instructed me to meet with you. I deal with PR, and I make the decisions around the Ryder centennial celebrations."

God, even her voice was sexy, containing a hint of rasp and smoke.

"Nice to meet you, darlin'."

The *darlin'* pissed her off and lightning flashed in her honey-whiskey eyes. He watched her run elegant fingers through her short, bright blond hair. It took a certain amount of confidence to wear her hair so short, but with her high cheekbones, straight nose and cat-like eyes, she pulled it off.

"You can call me Kinga or Ms. Ryder White but can the darlin's, *darlin'*."

Because he always preferred sass to subservience, Griff smiled. He wanted to ruffle her very proper feathers, so he added some extra drawl to his next words.

"I don't object to you calling me darlin', but if we must be formal, then you can call me Griff," he said, his voice sounding rusty.

What was happening here? Why was he reacting like this?

He'd met princesses and supermodels, A-list actresses and B-list bombshells—slept with a number of them—and none of them had managed to scramble his brains or twist his stomach and tongue into knots. Yet this woman, in charge of PR for her grandfather's company, did.

And he couldn't work out why.

"Would you like coffee or a soft drink?" Kinga said, sounding brisk and businesslike.

Griff glanced at his watch, saw it was after four forty-five and decided he needed a drink. He looked at the collection of whiskeys behind the bar. "Whiskey, single malt. Preferably something old."

"This is a business meeting. Coffee, water or something soft?" Kinga asked through obviously gritted teeth. Damn, annoying her was fun. He liked the way she looked down her nose at him, how those extraordinary eyes flashed with disdain. For the first time in…well, forever, Griff understood the lure of the chase.

Keeping his eyes on her lovely face, he lifted his hand and, as expected, a waiter immediately glided across the room to where they sat. Griff ordered a dram of expensive Macallan Royal Marriage, neat, and asked Kinga whether she'd like to join him.

To his surprise, Kinga nodded, her eyes not leaving his. He instinctively understood that they were jostling for control and direction of this conversation and it was a battle he wanted to win.

So did she.

Despite their eye contact, Kinga's expression remained impassive and Griff found himself intrigued by her ability to ignore their attraction. He'd recognized her bolt-from-the-blue response to him. But she'd pushed it down and away, acting like it never happened.

Interesting.

God, how long had it been since he had to work to impress a woman? Fifteen years? Twenty? Maybe never?

Kinga Ryder-White was the most intriguing—and possibly exasperating—woman he'd ever met.

They sat in silence, neither prepared to look away, until the waiter delivered their drinks, the liquid in the cut crystal glasses the same shade as her eyes. Kinga lifted the glass, took a sip and delicately placed her glass on the table between them.

"Ready to talk business?" she demanded, tapping her finger against her tablet. "Is your agent here with you?" Kinga added. "Your manager?"

"No," Griff briskly replied. He had major trust issues and, after Finn's betrayal, he was taking his time finding someone to represent him. The Ryder-White gig was an offer Griff could negotiate himself, especially since he hadn't decided whether to make his comeback permanent yet.

"Why didn't you sign with someone else after Finn Barclay died?" Kinga asked, taking another sip of her whiskey. He'd expected her to take a slug to make a point, but she seemed to be enjoying the expensive drink.

Griff saw the curiosity on her face and released a frustrated sigh. He hated talking about Finn. To this day, nobody else knew Finn had died in a car accident because he was racing to the ranch to confront

Griff about his decision to terminate their long relationship. Finn's treachery had taught him that the only person he could fully rely on was himself.

Eviscerated by how his association with Finn had ended, he doubted he could ever trust someone, anyone, again. It was why he'd stopped dating and why he was taking his time signing an agreement with another manager or agent.

"Well?" Kinga asked, tipping her head to the side, looking a little impatient at his lack of a reply.

Something made him want to tell her about Finn and Sian, about what had led him to this point. The impulse annoyed him. He never confided in anyone and God knew why he wanted to spill his soul to this uppity, in-your-face, sexy-as-sin female.

"None of your business," Griff told her, and he heard the annoyance in his own voice. That was okay, he was sure she could take it.

"Well, agents are the firewall between the artist and the client." Kinga handed him a smile that was part sweet, part sly. "It's so much easier to be frank with an agent than with the artist."

"I'm a big boy. I can handle it." He flashed a grin, enjoying the bite in her words, in her attitude.

Kinga acknowledged his words with a tilt of her head. She linked her fingers together, her gaze direct when her eyes met his. "My grandfather, Callum, seems to think you would be perfect to perform at the Ryder International ball. He likes the idea of being the one to relaunch you."

He considered telling Kinga the Ryder ball was

just a venue, that he had other venues, other options to consider. He'd wasn't desperate, for God's sake. He didn't *need* to do the concert, to return to the stage.

One option would be to simply sell his songs to other artists, but singing, performing and entertaining had been his entire life, starting with his first role alongside his twin, Sian, in an extremely popular sitcom when they were seven. At eighteen, they both landed roles in the smash-hit musical, *Peter and Me,* and its popularity transformed them into international celebrities, with the soundtrack becoming the top-selling album for the next two years, going platinum four times.

Over the next decade, he'd run from project to project, enjoying having the world at his feet. Then his universe had fractured, and What Happened to Griff? became an oft-used headline as journalists tried to figure out why a hardworking, dedicated and easy-to-work-with artist had turned into a publicity-seeking monster.

Griff placed his ankle on his other knee and linked his hands on his flat stomach. He was sure he knew the answer to his next question but decided to ask it anyway. "So you don't think I am suitable? Why not?"

"You don't fit the image for my ball, and you're not who I want to perform in front of many of our friends, family, guests, clients and colleagues, both local and international. They have certain expectations of the entertainment.

"You have a shocking reputation and haven't performed for a while." Well, he'd asked for an explanation and he'd got it.

Kinga didn't drop her eyes and Griff respected her take-no-prisoners attitude. "I'll be honest with you, Mr. O'Hare. I think hiring you would be a mistake and I intend to change my grandfather's mind."

Callum seemed pretty set on him, so Griff shrugged, knowing his casual gesture would frustrate her. Griff couldn't fault her for not wanting to take a chance on him. If he was in her position, he'd also have reservations about hiring a musician who'd trashed hotel rooms, closed down clubs, left with a different girl every night, racked up speeding fines in his superpowerful Ducati, dabbled in drugs and had three different children by three different women— all falsely reported but widely believed.

Most of his bad boy behavior was bullshit, a carefully constructed manipulation of the media. It was a simple equation: if he acted out, the media's attention focused on him and they ignored Sian, allowing his sister to fade from view.

He couldn't blame anyone for the bad press. After all, being bad was what he'd set out to do. And because he did everything well, he'd exceeded his own expectations.

Surprisingly, being wild and reckless took an enormous amount of time and energy. And he was sick of being portrayed as an asshole. It wasn't who he was, and he was ready for something new. Maybe performing at the ball would start to sway public opinion. To claw back some respect.

"You're not going to challenge me on that?" Kinga demanded, obviously impatient with him for taking so long to respond.

Griff wanted to tell her that it was an act, a well-choreographed show, but this was a secret he'd take to his grave. Only his family and his two best friends, Stan and Ava Maxwell, knew he'd spent the past few years diverting press attention away from his twin. If his actions were divulged, the press would try and discover what she was trying to hide. And them writing about Sian and her problems would be disastrous.

The press had all but forgotten Sian—thank God—and it was finally the right time to stage a comeback.

"No."

"You're a talented artist, Mr. O'Hare, and you have the voice of an angel."

Damned with faint praise. "Thank you."

"Those weren't my words. I read that quote somewhere," Kinga told him on a dismissive shrug. "Music isn't my thing. I can't hold a tune or keep a beat."

A million neurons in his brain died at the thought. "Everybody can hold the beat and sing a little," he protested.

"I'm music-impaired," Kinga assured him, waving a hand. "Anyway, that's beside the point. What I do know is PR, and hiring you would not be a good move for Ryder International. Unfortunately for me, my grandfather disagrees and thinks you are the bee's knees."

Her dismissive attitude shouldn't hurt—he'd heard worse over the years—but it still managed to prick his steel-hard hide. Damn her. Because he refused to let her see that her words had hit their target, he did what he normally did and resorted to flippancy.

"I often think about God and what he must've been thinking when He created bees," Griff mused, purely to wind her up. With her boss-girl demeanor, she radiated confidence and control and he was desperate to rattle her. "I can just imagine Him saying… give them the ability to make a substance that never spoils, a little sting and cute antennae. Oh, and give them kick-ass knees."

He thought he caught a hint of irritated humor but it flashed too quickly for him to be sure. She stared at him before shaking her head. "Are you done?"

"Probably not."

Kinga rolled those gorgeous eyes. "As I was saying, my grandfather thinks that being talked about— whether in a good or a bad light—is always better than not being talked about at all." She wrinkled her nose as if she were unable to believe anyone could be hoodwinked in such a way.

"I don't follow that school of thought. An association between Ryder and you is not in our best interests."

Another verbal blow. By the end of this conversation, he was going to look like a well-used punch bag.

"How did I come to your grandfather's notice?" Griff asked the question that had puzzled him from the moment he'd received Callum's first email raising the possibility of him performing at their ball.

Griff had no idea how Ryder-White obtained his private email address or how the man knew he was contemplating a comeback. He'd only shared that news with select people within the industry, and Callum Ryder-White had to have awesome connections, and deep pockets, to access that type of information. Griff wasn't sure whether to be pissed or pleased.

Performing at the intimate event—a ball for two thousand people was still a small gig—would be a good way to slide back into performing, to dip his toe into that always turbulent body of water. Along with returning to performing, he was also, finally, writing songs again, and was considering releasing a new album. But all these decisions had consequences, including increased press attention.

His return to work would also mean leaving Sian and her son for months at a time. He didn't know if that was a viable option.

"My grandfather adores Vinnie D'Angelo. The famous opera singer?"

Yeah, he knew who Vinnie was, had met him a couple of times, and genuinely liked the old guy. That was why he'd done a cover of "Nessun Dorma," Vinnie's favorite song, from the opera Turandot, for his eightieth birthday. That and because the piece was, instrumentally and vocally, a challenge...

"He saw the video you recently released and wasn't disappointed," Kinga explained.

Wow, that was a hell of a backhanded compliment. "Most people thought I nailed it."

"My grandfather has higher standards than most," Kinga replied, her smile a little flippant. She waved her words away, looking impatient. "Anyway, he saw that your fans are desperate for your return to performing—" Her expression suggested that she couldn't fathom why and the thought made him smile. He had no idea why her dismissive attitude amused him, but it did. "—and he figured it would be a publicity coup to have you perform at the ball."

"But you don't feel that way."

She widened her eyes, trying and failing to look innocent. "Whatever gave you that idea?"

His mouth twitched as he tried not to smile.

It took everything not to give her a big-ass, 'got you', smile. "Then, *darlin'*, you have a huge problem because your grandfather has already offered me the gig.

"But I never sign anything or agree to take on a project before meeting the people with whom I'll be working," he added.

She worked hard to contain her shock, but she recovered quickly, determination quickly replacing the annoyance in her eyes. "I'd prefer to book someone with a little less charisma and a great deal more reliability," she informed him, her voice six degrees cooler.

He heard her unspoken words… *Selfish, childish, out-of-control*.

The words, and the implication, so often repeated

in the press, hit him like another gut punch. His amusement faded and it took all his effort to keep his expression genial. He wasn't the type to spill his soul, but again he felt the urge to explain himself. To explain that the person she saw wasn't who he was. He wanted to tell her that the bad boy act was just that, an act, and he was so damn sick of being seen as problematic. All he wanted to do was write music, perform, be himself again.

Why her and why now? She was prim, buttoned-up, haughty and direct, but Griff had the uncomfortable sensation she was the only one who could get him to spill his secrets.

Despite his attraction to her, Griff knew he should get up and walk—hell, run—away. He'd find another way to stage his comeback. He instinctively knew this woman was dangerous, to his heart and his mind.

But he also needed this gig, not for the money—he had enough for ten lifetimes—but because music was what he did, and being a performer was who he was. He'd been someone else for so long…that he wanted this opportunity to be himself.

He'd sacrificed his reputation, his music and his career for his sister and her son, and now that she was stronger, he was ready to come back. Performing at the Ryder International charity ball was a good move for him, a classy move. A good, tasteful, move.

Suddenly, horribly, he was no longer convinced that he held the upper hand here.

Not because she was being difficult and not because she wasn't enthusiastic about him performing but because…

Crap. He ran a hand over his face.

…Because something about this woman resonated with him. She was a melody he had to put lyrics to, an unwritten song hovering on the edge of his subconscious.

She was a new instrument he'd yet to master, a song he'd yet to sing. A score that needed to be notated…

Damn. He was in serious trouble here.

# Two

Kinga stared at him, her fists bunched, cold with shock and dismay.

Because really, there was no way she'd heard him right. There was no way he *already* had an offer, because she'd explained to her grandfather, in precise detail, why hiring Griff was a terrible idea. Callum was hardheaded but he wasn't stupid...

Could the stubborn old goat have done this? Already made the deal? Set her up? Would he really put her in such a tenuous and unacceptable situation? Sure, he wouldn't have thought twice about it.

What the hell was she going to do?

And why the hell did her heart triple-thump and her lady parts thrum every time her eyes connected with Griff's?

He was a very good-looking guy, she accepted that. She liked his messy hair, square jaw covered with three-day-old stubble, his straight nose, the small scar on his right cheekbone. She knew, from pictures, that he had two delicious dimples, but despite his practiced smiles, she'd yet to see them.

His body was fantastic: wide shoulders and chest, a trim waist and big arms that strained the fabric of his expensive T-shirt. But it was his eyes that enthralled her. Kinga could lose herself in the deep green, the color of fir forests on a cold winter's day.

Highlighted by dark brows and thick lashes, they held a million secrets, none of them good. The thought occurred to her that his easy manner and relaxed demeanor lulled people into believing he was the devil-who-didn't-care, an unrepentant bad boy, but his eyes reflected an unexpected intelligence. They suggested there was a lot more to the man than his wild exploits.

Kinga gave her herself a mental slap and reminded herself that it didn't matter who or what O'Hare was; he wasn't suitable to be the headline act at *her* ball.

O'Hare performing at the ball would cause the press to sit up and take notice of the charity event, sure, and then Callum would take credit for being the visionary who'd given O'Hare a second chance *if* Griff behaved himself and turned in a decent performance.

If he messed up, Callum would blame her for the bad publicity, for hiring him. She'd be the one in the firing line. Family or not, Callum looked after himself first.

Kinga looked down at her bunched hand and released her cramping fingers. No, hiring Griff was too risky and she was risk averse. Bad things happened when she stuck her neck out and deviated from the norm. As she very well knew.

"So, to be clear, you haven't signed the contract yet?" Kinga asked, her voice, annoyingly, shaky.

"No, but I probably will. It's a classy event, a decent amount of people, and it's for charity, which will make me look good."

"Does that mean you are donating your fee?" Kinga demanded, leaning forward. Maybe she could make a little lemonade from lemons...

He grinned, white teeth flashing. "No, Ryder International will pay me for performing."

"Marvelous," Kinga muttered. *Jerk*. She sat back and folded her arms across her chest, vibrating with annoyance. "I intend to get my grandfather to change his mind."

"I think you know you won't," Griff told her, sounding amused, "but feel free to try.

"Oh, and good luck explaining to the press why you rescinded your offer to hire me," he added.

Kinga snapped her head up, her eyes colliding with his. "What the hell do you mean by that?"

"If you make this process difficult, I will send a press release to the mainstream media, telling them that I am thrilled to announce my comeback, starting with a performance at your ball."

Kinga linked her hands together and squeezed. "You can't do that without my permission!"

Griff leaned forward, his gaze intense. "Understand this, Ms. Ryder-White. I do not need your damn permission to do or say anything. I received an offer from the head of your organization, with a contract for the gig. I am going to accept that offer. This is my career, not yours."

"But it's my ball, dammit!" Kinga hotly replied. "And I'm pretty sure you don't want to work with me."

"If you become too annoying, I'll ask Callum to make someone else my liaison. Callum mentioned your temper and suggested I might prefer to work with your sister."

Tinsley was sweet, nice, quiet. And how stupid was it that she felt hurt at hearing Callum's words on Griff's lips. She looked down at the table and hoped he hadn't noticed her expression.

"Look at me, Kinga."

Kinga reluctantly lifted her eyes to his, hoping hers held fire, not pain. Griff stared at her, his expression impassive. "I'm your headline act—you might as well get used to it. Callum wants me, and from what I've read, he normally gets what he wants."

He was, unfortunately, right. And once Callum made up his mind, there was little hope of changing it. And, like his rare collection of illuminated manuscripts, the ring that once belonged to Marie Antoinette and his rare 1953 Jaguar, Griff was another shiny object to collect, use and forget about. He'd get the praise and publicity for luring Griff back into the spotlight and he'd enjoy that momentary thrill. It didn't matter that hiring Griff might not be in Ryder International's best interests. It would be up to others, like her, to manage any potential fallout.

If Griff had a contract offer from Callum, then she was locked into having him as her headline act. Instead of arguing with him, she needed to switch gears and start thinking about how to manage the press, how to spin his comeback into positive publicity for Ryder International. To protect the company, her job and herself.

She'd have to draw up a whole new publicity campaign. But the first step, obviously, was to ensure that he didn't do anything asinine between now and Valentine's Day.

Kinga rested her arms on the table and locked eyes with him, hoping her expression looked as fierce as she felt. "I'll make you a deal."

"This should be interesting," he drawled, amusement lifting the corners of his mouth. Right, so she didn't intimidate him at all. *Great.*

"I will not fight Callum on this and, believe me, I could. It might take some time but he would, eventually, listen to me." No, he wouldn't, but O'Hare didn't need to know that. "And we can easily afford to break your contract, pay you for any inconvenience caused. As far as the bad publicity that would generate, I think that a lot of people would understand why we felt we couldn't afford to take a risk on you."

Kinga thought she saw a flash of pain cross his

face but it came and went so quickly she couldn't be sure. But she did have his attention and that was all that mattered. She'd push her agenda while she had the upper hand. She suspected she wouldn't retain it for long.

"I control the publicity, *all* the publicity, including how we frame the story of your comeback." Griff started to speak but Kinga jumped in before he could. "You don't have a manager anymore and my sources in the industry tell me you don't have a publicist, either. Consider my PR services part of your remuneration package."

"I am perfectly able to manage my publicity," Griff said, his voice dangerously soft.

Kinga snorted. "No, you're not. And since your comeback intersects with my ball, I'm going to be the one controlling that narrative." She drilled her finger into his muscular forearm and ignored the fire when she touched him. Her uncontrollable attraction to him was very damn inopportune. And annoying.

"All you need to do is behave yourself. And because I don't trust you to do that, you will relocate to Portland, Maine, where I live and where Ryder International has its headquarters so I can keep an eye on you."

"No," Griff countered. "If I make it to Portland, it will be because I *want* to be there and not because you issued a royal decree."

Kinga frowned at him, wondering if he knew that the local press called her and Tinsley Portland's princesses, or whether his off-hand comment was just a coincidence.

"I want you in Portland, it's where our business is based, where the Ryder-White's have lived for generations," Kinga stated, momentarily distracted by the interest in his eyes. God, he was want-to-jump-you-hot.

She wondered what he'd do if she put her mouth on his, whether the heat swirling between them would erupt into a firenado.

She rather suspected it would. The flames between them were sky-high and if he were anyone other than, well, *him*, she might be tempted to explore their crackling chemistry. Even to the point of suggesting they get a room...

The thought shocked her.

She wasn't an impulsive person. She didn't make quick decisions. Her impulsive behavior at the New Year's Eve party a decade ago had led to tragedy, so she analyzed everything, considered all options, worked all out the possible outcomes and consequences. Only then did she act.

"I want you to relocate to Portland," Kinga repeated her suggestion.

"That's not going to happen." Griff's insolent smile pulled her back to reality.

"Chin up, darlin'," he drawled. "I realize you are a boss girl, but not everyone is always going to fall into line with your wishes. Maybe I've been sent to remind you of that."

She'd never admit it to him, or anyone, that she

suspected he was right. That her vociferous opposition to Griff just made Callum more determined to have him perform. Callum liked shaking her up, making her feel off-balance and out of control. He liked the idea of his grandchildren working in the family business but would far prefer she and Tinsley were male.

Callum wasn't a fan of strong, successful women.

Mind games—Callum was a master at them. But she wouldn't let him, or any other man, get the better of her. Kinga forced herself to drop her shoulders, to send him a cool smile. "I think this whole process would run smoother if we worked together so I would greatly appreciate your presence in Portland, Mr. O'Hare."

Where she could keep her beady eye on him.

It galled her to admit that she'd lost this first battle between them—she had no doubt there would be many more—and she knew it was time to retreat. Picking up her tablet and bag, she slid out of the booth, a little surprised when Griff stood, too. The man, surprisingly, had manners...

"I need to leave now to catch my flight," she said, digging into the side pocket of her tote bag for a business card. She handed it over and watched him tuck it into the back pocket of his jeans. "I'll pick up the tab and let you go back to doing what you seem to do best."

"And that is?" Griff asked, laughter back in his eyes.

"Picking up random women in bars."

Griff dipped his head and Kinga had the wild thought that he was about to kiss her. She should step back, retreat, but her feet refused to cooperate. She wanted him to kiss her, she realized; she wanted to know how he tasted, whether his big body was as muscled as she expected.

Dear God, this wasn't good.

But instead of kissing her, Griff's warm, whiskey-tinged breath drifted over her cheek before stopping an inch from her ear.

"Just to be clear, I wasn't trying to pick up a random woman. I was trying to pick up *you*. See you soon, darlin'."

Kinga stared at his broad back as he walked away, wishing that she could give in to her impulse to throw the heavy crystal tumbler at his head.

Maybe she should just order another drink. She sure as hell could use one.

Feeling a little shaken, Griff strode across the lobby, helmet tucked under his arm. Looking around, he realized that instead of heading for the exit, he'd walked deeper inside, to a reception area dotted with comfortable couches and...

Holy crap, a Fazioli Aria.

Griff immediately crossed the harlequin floor to the piano and watched the pianist's elegant fingers dancing across the keys. She was young and pretty but all of his attention was on one of the most luxurious, insanely expensive pianos in the world. He was a Gibson guy, but he'd taken piano lessons and knew his way around the keyboard.

The redhead saw his approach, her eyes widening when she recognized him. To her credit, she didn't stumble or stop, but simply raised an eyebrow. Her mouth lifted into a half smile. "Griff O'Hare, hello. Do you play?"

Griff nodded. "Guitar is my first love but I've been known to lose hours massacring Mozart or Bach."

She segued into Henry Mancini's "Moon River" and her smile turned flirty. "Feel free to join in…"

Griff looked around and grimaced. That would attract more attention than he was looking for. "No, thanks. It's a beautiful instrument."

"They have another in the ballroom."

"Two Faziolis?" Be still, his beating heart.

"The owners of this place don't spare any expense. I'm Alice, by the way. Are you checking in?"

"I've just come from a meeting," Griff replied and internally grimaced at the flirtatious glint in her eye. He knew what was coming next—it was as predictable as the sun rising in the east.

Three, two, one…

"Would you like to meet with me as well? I'll be done in ten minutes."

He was such a freaking genius. "Thanks, but I can't," Griff told her, allowing his hand to skim over the upraised lid. "Nice meeting you, Alice."

Conscious of eyes following his progress across the lobby, he fought the urge to walk back into the

Ryder International bar situated in a prime position just off the main lobby and engage Kinga Ryder-White in some nonbusiness conversation.

*I-wonder-what-you-taste-like* and *I'm-desperate-to-see-you-naked* conversation. But her frosty looks and don't-go-there attitude told him he had more of a chance of becoming pregnant than he did of persuading her into his arms and his bed.

And maybe that was life's way of telling him he should put all his energy into this comeback performance. Deep in thought, Griff nearly ran into the back of a petite gray-haired lady. After muttering an apology, he stepped through the lobby doors and headed to where he'd parked his Ducati a few blocks away. He liked walking, and riding his loud and powerful bike up to the valet station was just asking for unneeded attention.

Jamming on a pair of sunglasses and a ball cap he'd tucked into the inner pocket of his jacket, he dodged tourists and New Yorkers, walking swiftly, still deep in thought.

His thoughts, as they often did, centered on his sister, his twin. It had been nearly ten years since the doctors first diagnosed Sian with schizophrenia, yet it felt like yesterday. Directly after the diagnosis, and because she'd wanted out of the industry, Sian had retreated to his horse ranch in Kentucky, shunning company and raising a lot of gossip in the press.

After some salacious speculation about his sister, Griff and his manager, Finn, had agreed that they needed to divert press attention from Sian. Finn accepted that Griff's transformation into a bad boy was the way to go. He also insisted that Griff embarking on a "Raising Hell" tour was necessary. Griff hadn't wanted to leave Sian, but Finn promised to look after his twin while Griff toured. Yet, while he was away, what Griff had believed to be a father-daughter relationship had turned sexual and Sian had gotten pregnant.

Griff still struggled to believe that the man he'd considered to be his second father—his parents had died when he and Sian were in their early twenties—and his mentor could have turned an avuncular relationship with Sian into something sexual, especially knowing how vulnerable his sister was.

*Bastard.*

Sian didn't see it the same way he did, and frequently told him that her liaison with Finn had been consensual, that she went into the affair with her eyes wide open. But Griff, deeply protective of his twin—to her immense frustration—couldn't help but think that Finn had taken advantage of her need for comfort and reassurance. Her need to feel normal and attractive and like the sexy woman she was before she was diagnosed.

A lot of advantage…

But, on the plus side, Griff had managed to keep the press away from all of Sian's private life. Nobody knew Finn was Sam's father, that Sian had mental health issues or that she was a mother. He'd managed to snow them all and that had been, after all, his primary objective. Given the same set of circumstances and presented with the same choices, he'd do it all over again.

She was his twin, the person he shared life with before life and he'd rearrange the heavens for her if so required.

Griff walked up to his bike, whipped off his cap and jammed on his helmet. Knowing he was well disguised, he straddled the bike and watched the passing traffic, both pedestrian and vehicular.

He'd do it all again, of course he would. He'd do anything to protect Sian and Sam and never considered them a burden or a drag.

But he was so damn sick of being portrayed as an attention-seeking publicity hound, the bad boy performer.

He'd once been respected as a consummate professional and he desperately wanted to restore his reputation. It was, he thought, the right time to do that. Sian was stable and the entertainment industry wasn't focused on her anymore. Sam was thriving. Griff was thirty-five years old and he'd been keeping a low profile lately—well, a lot lower than before—and this ball, elegant and exclusive, would set the tone for his comeback and whatever came next in his career.

He could do the concert, see how he was received, and then decide what path to follow.

And bonus, he'd be working with the stunningly sexy Kinga Ryder-White, she of the long, lanky body, short, bright blond hair. And eyes the color of secrets and sass.

Yeah, so far the Ryder International ball was turning out to be a damn good deal.

## Penelope

Watching from the windows of their private sitting room situated in one of the two wings of Callum's sprawling mansion, Penelope watched James walk up the path from the beach, his hair windblown and his cheeks pink with cold. But no matter the weather, whenever they came to Ryder's Rest, he'd take his to-go cup of coffee to the beach and spend some time staring at the sea.

Her husband was a creature of habit, Penelope thought. She liked that about him. Unlike her, James was an open book.

Penelope poured herself another cup of coffee and flipped open her crocodile-skin diary to check her schedule for today. She had Pilates at eleven, lunch with friends at one and a meeting with the Ryder Foundation CEO at four to discuss the many requests for funding and grants that the foundation regularly received. It was always hard to prioritize need and so many people needed their help...

Pen hoped she managed to concentrate long enough to make a meaningful contribution to the discussion.

Her thoughts, since doing that stupid DNA test, had been scattered and her attention span was mini-

mal. Picking up her coffee cup, she walked back over
to the window and stared down at Dead Man's Cove,
thinking back on her life and the choices she made.

And the consequences of those choices.

But in time, she'd learned to live with the guilt
and the emptiness, and she'd devoted herself to raising her two girls as best she could. Now in her late
fifties, Pen had thought that the past was far behind
her and that her secret was safe.

Callum's "gift" of a DNA test had flipped that
belief on its head.

Penelope heard James step into the room and
turned to look at him. His blond hair was tousled,
and he looked tired and stressed. No, she corrected,
James was always stressed. Working for his demanding and unappreciative father was difficult beyond
measure. He looked like his uncle, she realized with
a pang.

"Morning, Pen."

Penelope returned his subdued greeting. They
hadn't been in love when they married; the union
had been, to an extent, an arranged marriage. Her
parents were friends of the Ryder-Whites—and she'd
been considered suitable, rich, educated, and of the
right social class to join the Ryder-White clan. Callum never suspected she was anything other than another debutante in her early twenties, an educated,
innocent, wealthy man's daughter who had, like so
many of her friends, spent a year abroad.

But somehow, despite the massive secret she kept
from him, she and James had made their marriage

work, by becoming friends first, then lovers, then parents.

They'd raised two beautiful girls, and if James had had an affair, or a few, he'd been discreet. She wasn't emotional about her marriage or her husband, and fully expected him to stray: it was what men— her father included—did.

Her marriage was stable. They were rich, popular, respected…semi-famous. She didn't want anything to change and the secrets of her life before James to be revealed.

"Are you okay, Pen?" James asked, coming up to stand beside her.

Pen started to tell him she was fine, but on see- ing his worried eyes, shook her head. "Not really. Are you?"

James shrugged. Pen sighed, knowing James wasn't one to rock the boat. Her husband's sweet nature and his hatred of conflict were why Callum treated him like a servant. Her father-in-law was a bully, and like all bullies, he only respected people who stood up to him.

"Just tired," James lied. "I feel like I'm on a tread- mill and there's no getting off."

When she looked at him, she frowned at the emo- tion in his eyes. Working for his father had worn him down, and she wished, sometimes desperately, that they could run away, start again.

But unfortunately, some things followed you wherever you went.

James stared out the window, his square jawline

taut. With his thick blond hair turning silver, blue eyes and fit body, her husband was still a gorgeous man. She was lucky to be married to him, lucky to enjoy the fabulous lifestyle he provided, to be respected and even, occasionally, feted.

That could change…

No, it *would* change. It was best to be prepared.

Once a month, Callum insisted on a family meeting to be held around the two-hundred-year-old dining table at Ryder's Rest. After they were done discussing Ryder International and Ryder-White business, they adjourned to Callum's reception room to drink sherry while his housekeeper set the dining table for a four-course dinner followed by port and, if they felt so inclined, a hand of cards or a game of billiards.

It was all very Downton Abbey. Every family member's attendance was mandatory and, being so busy, Kinga and Tinsley chafed at the wasted time and mentally mocked their grandfather's pretensions.

He was not a bloody duke or a member of the peerage. This wasn't aristocratic England, for God's sake.

But because no good ever came of rocking the boat, Kinga gritted her teeth, drank his revolting sherry and followed Tinsley to her seat at the dining table where they'd discuss business over dinner.

Tinsley glanced around, and seeing that her grandfather was preoccupied at the other end of the room with pouring himself another whiskey, nudged

Kinga with her elbow. "You're looking very militant, Kingaroo. What's up?"

"A thousand and one things," Kinga muttered, flipping open the cover to her iPad. Not least of which was the fact that she couldn't stop thinking about that man-devil, Griff O'Hare. He popped into her thoughts all the time and then she spent a few minutes remembering the color of his eyes, the width of his shoulders, the way his jeans cupped his very nice package...

Dear God, she was losing her mind.

"Whose stupid idea was it to have a yearlong celebration of everything Ryder International?" she demanded, sounding irritated.

Her dad stopped next to her seat and dropped a kiss on her head. "Yours, darling."

Kinga twisted her lips. "And, except for the notion of hiring O'Hare to sing at the ball, it was the stupidest idea ever."

Tinsley sent her a sympathetic look and jerked her chin. Kinga turned her head to see Callum approaching his chair at the head of the table. He'd exchanged his suit jacket for one of his many vintage smoking jackets, this one a rich burgundy with black velvet lapels. Callum sat down, opened his leather folder and picked up his Montblanc fountain pen, one of only six made in the world. The unlined paper on which he made notes was handcrafted and his whiskey glass was made in Bohemia. Callum was a blue blood and nothing but the best was good enough for him.

Griff was annoying, sure, but at least the man wasn't pretentious. And why was she thinking about him?

Callum cleared his throat and his pale blue eyes landed on James. "Why have you made no progress in establishing who owns the block of shares that are out of my control?"

James gave his father the same answer he did every time he was asked this question. "Callum, the shares are held in a trust. The trust is confidential." James lifted up his hand. "All we can do is send letters—as we have been doing—via the trustee's lawyers and hope he responds. If he doesn't, our hands are tied."

Callum released a low growl. "What the hell was Benjamin thinking leaving those shares to someone out of the family?"

*Ah, that might be because you, Callum, flipped out when he told you he was in love with another man.* Karma, as she'd learned, never lost an address or failed to deliver.

Kinga caught Tinsley's eye and rolled her own.

"Would it help to hire a private investigator to look into Benjamin's life at the time that he bequeathed the shares?" Callum demanded.

Kinga saw frustration in her father's eyes. "We did that, and the only person close to Ben at the time was the man he briefly lived with, the man he wanted to marry." James shook his head at Callum's look of distaste. Unlike Callum, her parents were tolerant and accepting. They'd taught her and Tinsley that love was love.

"I had the PI dig into his life, but Carlos lived simply, a solidly upper-middle-class life. If he had access to Ben's wealth, he would've at least paid off his mortgage. He didn't. The investigator found no indication that Carlos controls those shares, but we don't know who else might."

"Can we please move on?" Penelope demanded.

Kinga frowned at her mom's terse tone. "Mom? Are you okay?"

"We keep beating the same dead horse! The shares are out of our reach. Maybe it's time to accept that!" Penelope muttered.

Callum narrowed his eyes at his daughter-in-law. "If I simply accepted what I was told, I would not own a ten-billion-dollar company, Penelope. You would not be wearing Chanel or sporting a five-carat diamond or driving the latest BMW."

Penelope pushed her fingertips into her eye sockets. "Yes, I understand, Callum. Sorry."

*Stop apologizing, Mom! You didn't do anything wrong.* Kinga shook her head. She saw the glint in her grandfather's eye as he looked at her mom's bent head, the small smile on his lips.

Callum loved putting people in their place; he got a kick out of knocking people down, especially women. So why was she still working for the man? Why didn't she just leave?

Kinga sighed. Because, while she didn't like her grandfather, she loved the business, loved her demanding and interesting job and she thought that, maybe, she could draw some of Callum's fire from her father.

"I sent you a copy of Griff O'Hare's signed contract, Callum," Kinga said, wanting to move the meeting along. Damn, even saying his name made her feel squidgy, off balance. What was wrong with her?

Callum scowled at her, and Kinga knew he was debating whether to scold her for hijacking his agenda. "I saw that. And I am pleased with the publicity his comeback has generated."

So was she...for now. "But if they'd spend a little more time talking about the ball and the Ryder Foundation and less about Griff O'Hare's exploits, I'd be grateful," Kinga said.

"I'm still being touted as the person who persuaded him to come out of retirement, so I have no issue with the press coverage," Callum told her.

Of course, he didn't. But when O'Hare messed up, Callum would throw Kinga to the press wolves. Despite frequently telling the world that his family meant everything to him, her grandfather always put himself first.

"I have some ideas about the songs I want O'Hare to sing," Callum stated.

Kinga swallowed her groan. She and Griff had exchanged at least a dozen emails arguing about who had creative control over his set list, with him threatening to walk unless she butted out. So she'd butted out.

Now Callum, who obviously hadn't read the contract, wanted to butt back in.

"That's not going to happen, Callum. Griff won't tolerate any interference with his creative control of the performance," Kinga told him, enjoying his shocked expression. In Griff, Callum might just have found someone equally stubborn. The thought amused her. And turned her on.

Honestly? Everything about O'Hare turned her on.

"That's not acceptable. I will have my way."

"Not this time you won't," Kinga shot back. "If you interfere, he walks and we don't have a performer."

"Who the hell drew up that damn contract?" Callum shouted, his face flushed with temper.

Kinga leaned back in her chair and smiled. "You did, Callum. I sent you a memo detailing my concerns, and control of his set list was one of them. I was surprised to see that you signed it with no alterations."

"I…what…how—" Callum blustered.

Tinsley kicked her ankle and Kinga's smile faded. Right, baiting the bear was never a clever tactic.

"Have you received the DNA tests back yet, Callum?" Tinsley asked him, changing the subject yet again. Kinga sent her a grateful smile.

"This family seems to forget that I have an agenda to follow," Callum retorted. "But to answer your question, no, I have not. The laboratory sent me an email telling me that there was a snafu and our results would be delayed."

"All of them?" James asked. Kinga heard the note of doubt in his voice and didn't blame him. She could understand there being a problem with one sample but five? At the same time?

"Must we swipe the inside of our mouths again, Callum?" James asked.

"I would've told you if that was what was required."

Kinga pulled a face at Callum's terse tone and hauled in a series of calming breaths. It was going to be a long meeting and an even longer evening.

# Three

Two weeks had passed since Kinga and Griff's initial flurry of email-based arguments about the set list and publicity. Despite reaching out via emails, text messages and leaving messages on his voice mail, Kinga hadn't heard a squeak out of him in over ten days.

She needed to talk to the man. She needed to discuss the ball, press releases, interviews…

She also wanted to know whether she'd seen sadness flicker across his face or simply imagined the sexual interest she saw in his eyes.

She couldn't stop thinking about him, wondering what he was doing, whom he was with…

Kinga shook her head, surprised at the fast, hot flame of jealousy travelling across her skin. She'd met him once—one time!—and he had her acting like an idiot.

God knew what would happen if she spent more time with him.

Sitting in the corner of her comfortable couch, Kinga closed the report she'd been reading and moved her machine from her lap to the coffee table in front of her. She pulled her feet up onto the couch and wrapped her arms around her knees, her eyes invariably drifting toward the heavy silver frame on the mantel of her fireplace.

The photo was taken a week or two before Jas died. They'd spent a weekend skiing Saddleback Mountain and they'd asked a cute ski instructor to take their photograph. Their noses were pink from the cold, their eyes sparkling, their smiles boldly declaring that they were young, beautiful and invincible.

Jasmine had been a ray of sunshine, could make friends with a lamppost and, within a day of reaching the ski resort, knew a dozen people by name. She was the eternal optimist, a free spirit, someone thoroughly in love with life. The daughter of a prominent senator and his equally charismatic wife, Jas had been born with confidence, ebullience and the ability to persuade a rock to crumble. They'd met in kindergarten, bonded immediately and, with them both attending the same exclusive private school, forged an unbreakable friendship.

Determined, intensely bright and vivacious, Jas pulled Kinga, reserved and a little shy, out of her shell, and it was because of Jas that she had a social life.

Jas made her braver and bolder.

Then Jas died...

Kinga wished she could remember Jas without having to recall the soul-destroying events that occurred a decade before. But that was impossible and her mind wandered down that all too familiar, dark path.

*It's all good, Kingaroo, I'll be fine.*

Kinga sighed at the sound of Jas's voice in her head. It hadn't been good and nothing was fine.

The memories were as vivid today as they'd ever been. Kinga could still recall the fear in Jas's mom's voice when she called on the first day of the new year. She'd asked whether Jas had slept over at her house, because she hadn't returned home that night. She remembered rushing to the Garwood house and screaming at the police officers, trying to get them to believe Jas wasn't a runaway, that she hadn't left home for places unknown. Walking Cousin's Island, paralyzed with fear as she papered windows, poles and cars with missing-person flyers.

Stopping now and again to cry and pray her heart out for Jas's swift return. Wishing she'd never left Jas at that party...

A few days later they found her body, lying under snow in a ditch on the side of the road. The police determined it was a hit-and-run and the culprit had never been identified.

Jas's on-off boyfriend, Mick Pritchard—the boy who grew up next door to Kinga and whom she'd known even longer than she'd known Jas—told her, and anybody who would listen, that she was to blame for Jas's death.

He was right.

Kinga placed her face in her hands, desperately wishing she'd hung around and given Jas a lift home as she'd promised she would. That instead of leaving with some long forgotten boy, she'd stayed, seeing in the new year with her best friend.

Kinga reached for her wine, draining the last inch in one long swallow.

She was still close to Jas's parents but the loss of their daughter had changed them in ways that were almost impossible to understand. Her father, Seth, still served as Maine's senator but, to Kinga, it was like the light within him had dimmed. Viola, Jas's mom, rarely left their sprawling estate.

Kinga missed Jas but she also missed the loving, fun people who'd once been Jas's parents. But thankfully, they'd never blamed her for what happened that night.

Unlike Mick, who was relentless in his attacks. He'd confronted her after the funeral and, over the past ten years, on each anniversary of Jas's death, he sent her either a text message, a voice message or an email, sometimes all three, reminding her that Jas would be alive if it weren't for her actions. And he always, always sent her the link to the sales video on his company website…

*"When I was twenty, I lost the love of my life, Jas Garwood, Senator Garwood's only daughter, in a hit-and-run accident. Her best friend, Kinga Ryder-White, was supposed to see her home from a New Year's party and failed to do so. Jas chose to walk and, in the mist and rain, was hit by a vehicle. I have chosen to dedicate my life to helping others by providing security services."*

She didn't need Mick's reminders. She lived with the consequences of her actions every single day. She had not only lost her best friend, but she was the reason the Garwoods had lost their only child.

Jas's death had changed Kinga, too. She never, ever allowed herself to act rashly, seldom made new friends or dated. She analyzed every decision she made, overthought everything.

And she'd vowed she would never voluntarily love someone so much again.

She loved Tinsley and her parents—but loving your family was baked in from birth, wasn't it? To voluntarily love, or to fall in love, meant taking the risk of letting someone down, making another mistake. Being hurt.

She would never allow that to happen again.

Knowing that she had to stop thinking about Jas, Kinga jumped up and turned the silver frame to face the wall. The memories and regrets were strong tonight, and not seeing Jas's laughing face might keep her thoughts from returning to that awful time so long ago.

She needed to think of something else, someone else.

She could think about Griff O'Hare…

*Like you weren't thinking about him just ten minutes ago.*

Annoyed with that mocking inner voice, Kinga walked over to her window and placed her hand on the pane, idly watching the wicked weather outside. It was snowing, again, and the weather people were predicting another winter storm to roll in later.

She wondered how Griff, when he finally dragged himself to Portland, would cope with their weather. She knew he owned an island off the Florida Keys, a ranch in Kentucky, houses in Malibu and Nashville, apartments in Manhattan and London, but she didn't know which of his many properties was his primary residence.

If she did, she'd find him and drag him back to Portland by his hair, cave girl style.

They needed to finalize the PR strategy, but let's be honest here, she couldn't wait to look into his forest green eyes, to watch for those sexy dimples, to hear his deep drawl saying her name. Kinga sighed. She couldn't believe she was at risk of falling under the spell of a bad boy.

Nothing was going to happen between them, Kinga told herself as a big SUV turned the corner into her street.

She turned away from the window, reminding herself that she didn't make connections, take risks, make impulsive moves.

It wasn't what she did, who she was.

* * *

Griff pulled up to the third of four redbrick buildings on Congress Street and turned off the engine to his rented Mercedes SUV. Placing his arms on the steering wheel, he looked up at the imposing building with its stained glass inserts above the front door, the original slate roof and tall chimneys.

He looked to the right and noticed the discreet signage indicating that the property next door was a boutique hotel.

It looked glamorous and expensive and Griff wasn't surprised that the granddaughter of the town's richest man lived here. It was perfectly situated, smack bang in the arts district, and he'd noticed many upmarket restaurants and trendy shops nearby. It was also a short walk to Portland's famous harbor.

From the little he'd seen from his after-dinner stroll earlier, he rather liked this small, vibey, unpretentious city. He liked the Old Port, an appealing old harbor town with amazing architecture and cobblestone sidewalks. He'd never visited this part of the world before but knew that spending time here wouldn't be a hardship.

Admittedly, Kinga Ryder-White was, for him, one of the city's main attractions.

Leaving his vehicle, Griff pulled his jacket off the back of the driver's seat and shrugged it on, trying and failing to ignore the icy splatters hitting his hair, face and shoulders. If he was going to stay in Maine any length of time, he was going to have to buy himself a big-ass umbrella. After locking his car, he walked across the road—being careful to avoid puddles—and strode up the steps to stand under the portico at the entrance to the building. There were only three apartments—K Ryder-White and T Ryder-White lived in apartments A and B, while C didn't have a name attached—and Griff jammed his finger on the buzzer of the apartment belonging to Kinga.

"Yes?"

It was one word but he heard the fear in her voice. He should've given her some warning that he was coming over but he'd landed in Portland just a few hours before, grabbed some food and decided he couldn't wait until morning to see her. She'd been on his mind since he left Manhattan.

A most unusual circumstance.

"It's Griff O'Hare."

"What the hell? It's after eleven, O'Hare." Kinga told him, sounding pissy. Man, he loved her irritated rasp.

"You've left at least two dozen messages telling me to get in touch." Griff smiled, his forearm resting on the wall above his head. He grinned, enjoying the fact he could rile her so easily. "This is me, getting in touch."

"This is you, being a pain in my ass," Kinga shot back.

Griff chuckled, loving her sass. "Apparently, we've got lots to discuss, so let me in, darlin'. It's colder than a witch's—"

Kinga interrupted him to mutter something indistinguishable but definitely uncomplimentary. He grinned when her door clicked open.

Griff walked into the pretty lobby dominated by an old, intricate chandelier. It was a small area and he couldn't help wondering what happened to the wooden staircase that would've once dominated the space. The U-shaped lobby held three identical, and old, wooden doors, a small lemon tree in an ornamental pot and a wooden bench with plump black-and-white cushions.

He turned to knock on Kinga's door but before he could, she opened it, standing there in a pair of men's-style flannel pajamas, in a pretty mint-and-white check. She wore chunky socks on her feet, her short hair was messy and her face free of makeup.

She looked, as Sian used to say, *uh-maz-zing*.

"It's late, O'Hare," Kinga said, leaning her shoulder against the wooden doorframe. "Go away and we'll meet in the morning."

Griff glanced at his watch and shrugged. "You weren't sleeping," he pointed out. She might look like she was ready for bed but she didn't look remotely sleepy. Griff suspected she'd been working when he leaned on her buzzer.

Griff turned at the sound of a door opening behind him and in that doorway stood a gorgeous woman with long, straight, coal black hair, pale, creamy skin and navy blue eyes. Sexy as hell, but she didn't nudge his I'm-attracted-to-her needle. However, the whiskey-eyed beauty with the sharp tongue, still glaring at him, sent it revving into the red zone.

"Griff O'Hare, meet my sister, Tinsley."

Tinsley, dressed in blue jeans, thick socks and a cable-knit sweater, mirrored her sister's pose against the doorframe and uttered a cool, "Hello."

"It is ridiculously late, Mr. O'Hare," Tinsley stated. Like her sister, she was equally unimpressed with his late-night visit. And with him.

Griff looked from one sister to the other and shrugged. "On the West Coast, we normally only start our evening around about now."

"And get up at noon," Kinga snapped. "Some of us have real jobs that start early."

She had no idea of the time and effort it took to reach his one-time level of success. Rising early, hitting the gym, learning lines, filming, rehearsing or recording. When one worked fourteen- or sixteen-hour days, the only time to socialize was from eleven onward.

He wanted to defend himself, something he hadn't had the urge to do in a very long time. Damn, that was the second time he wanted to explain and had no doubt it wouldn't be the last.

He returned his gaze to Kinga and saw she was looking past him to Tinsley. The two sisters seemed to be having a silent but intense conversation.

What was he missing here? Whatever they were discussing, they gave off enough of a vibe to make him feel he'd overstepped. He raised his hands and put some distance between himself and Kinga's door. "You're right, it's late. We can meet in the morning."

He turned to Tinsley to tell her that it was nice to

meet her and caught her shocked expression when Kinga ordered him, "Come on in."

"Would you like me to join you, make coffee or something?" Tinsley asked, her eyes not leaving her sister's face.

Kinga sent her a soft smile. "No, we're good. Thanks, Tins."

Tinsley's eyes widened again in surprise and Griff knew he was missing a lot of subtext. He didn't like it.

He started to demand an explanation but then remembered he hated people asking him personal questions, so he pushed down his curiosity.

After nodding to Tinsley, he walked into Kinga's apartment and heard the door shut behind him. Turning, he saw Kinga eyeing the four locks on her door, as if trying to decide whether to lock them or not. Four locks? Wasn't that excessive?

A thought occurred, one that burned a hole in his stomach. "Are you scared of me?" he demanded.

Kinga slowly turned, and when she faced him, she cocked her head to the side, as if trying to figure out her answer. Griff held his breath, waiting for her reply. If she was even remotely uneasy, he'd leave.

One hint of hesitation and he was gone.

A soft smile passed through Kinga's lovely eyes but Griff knew it wasn't directed at him. "I'm not," she said, sounding amused. "You annoy me and irritate me but, surprisingly, you don't scare me."

Okay. Well, good.

Kinga released a tiny chuckle and brushed past

him. His nose filled with her scent, something light and subtle and thoroughly sexy. It wasn't perfume... shower soap, maybe? Shampoo?

Disconcerted, Griff followed her into her open-plan living, dining, kitchen area. A staircase was to his right, and her walls were covered with abstract works of art that were both playful and thought-provoking. Cream couches holding bright, jewel-colored cushions sat next to the bay window, and he looked through the glass coffee table to the Persian rug tossed over the old hardwood floor. The back wall of the kitchen was exposed red brick.

There were fresh flowers on a side table and roses in a round glass bowl on the mantel next to an ornate silver frame, its face to the wall. He frowned. What was up with that?

Griff looked around and whistled. "This place is fantastic."

Kinga padded over to the kitchen and turned her slim back on him to take two fat wineglasses from a slim cupboard next to a stainless steel fridge. "Thanks. My dad dabbles in real estate and he found this place and converted it into three apartments. As you noticed, Tinsley is opposite me and there's a much smaller third apartment behind us both. We bought the building from my dad a few years back."

"And I presume you rent the other apartment?" Griff said, taking off his coat and draping it over the back of the closest sofa.

Kinga poured red wine into two glasses, her shoulders lifting in a small shrug. "The hotel next door occasionally rents the apartment from us if they have a family group they can't accommodate. It's fully furnished, so it works for both of us."

Griff took the glass she held out and when her fingers brushed against his, he felt the unmistakable current of attraction run up his arm. Judging by the way her eyes widened, she was feeling it, too.

Good to know. And bad to explore because they were about to commence their working relationship.

Griff knew engaging in a physical relationship would be a lot more fun. And satisfactory.

Kinga placed her glass on the coffee table and shifted from foot to foot, her eyes going to the stairway. "Can you give me five minutes? I'd like to change into something a little less informal."

"Don't bother on my account," Griff told her, sitting down at the end of her comfortable sofa. He placed his ankle on his knee and took a sip of the wine, sighing at its complexity. Like her taste in buildings and interior decor, Kinga's taste in wine was exquisite.

"Nice. What am I drinking?"

Kinga hesitated before perching on the sofa opposite his and lifting her wineglass to her lips. She sniffed, took a sip and sighed. "Ah, this is a bottle of 2005 Vieux Château Certan."

"It reminds me of Château Pétrus from the same year."

Kinga smiled. "It's supposed to. My dad is a wine buff and he has a case of the Pétrus. He won't waste the truly excellent stuff on Tinsley and me—apparently our palates aren't sophisticated enough—so he finds reasonable alternatives for us." Kinga crossed her legs and placed her elbow on her knee and her chin in her hand. "Are you a wine connoisseur?"

He had, so he'd been told, one of the best wine cellars in the country and, like whiskey, he enjoyed a glass of the good stuff. But never more than one or two. Drinking too much and too often was like flirting with a very slippery slope and he preferred to avoid the fall. Griff shrugged. "I like wine."

Kinga's direct gaze didn't drop from his face. She sipped again before nailing him with a hard look. "Why are you here, O'Hare?"

He couldn't tell her that she'd been on his mind constantly, that every time he saw an email from her, or a text message, or heard an increasingly irate voice message, he fought the urge to drop everything and fly out to her. That no other woman had ever taken up so much of his mental energy and that when he saw her standing in her doorway, dressed in her cute pj's, he'd felt like he'd taken his first proper breath since leaving New York City.

That waiting until morning to see her had been impossible…

Griff pushed his hand through his damp hair and took a huge gulp of wine. He didn't know what was happening here, but he had to get his thoughts under control. He wasn't looking for a partner, or a significant other or even, right now, a part-time lover. Sex would be great, but not if it came with complications, and Kinga embodied the word.

"You told me you wanted to see me," Griff eventually responded, keeping his face bland.

"Our conversation could've waited until the morning."

Griff couldn't pull his gaze off her lovely brown eyes and his heart rate picked up. What was it about this woman? Why did she make his extremities tingle, his mouth dry, and, yeah, his cock harden? She wasn't the most beautiful woman he'd ever laid eyes on. She was definitely the bossiest. But he still found himself constantly thinking about her, wanting to know what made her smile, what made her sigh.

He sipped his wine, slid down farther in the seat and rested the back of his head against the back of her couch. Her apartment was warm, she was pretty to look at and he had a glass of red in his hand. His home life was in order. His nephew, Sam, was his happy self. His sister, Sian, was stable, and Eloise, his former au pair and now his right hand, had everything under control.

He could relax. Just a little.

"Tell me about the ball," Griff suggested and smiled when she scooted back in her seat and tucked her feet under her butt. She held her wineglass to her chest, but her eyes lit up at the question. It was obvious the project was important to her.

"The ball is to be held in six weeks, on February fourteenth, as you know."

"If you're planning on a red-and-white theme with a million hearts, I might throw up," Griff told her. He couldn't think of anything more obvious.

Kinga released a little snort. "Please, I have better taste than that. The nod to Valentine's Day will be very subtle—Belgian chocolate hearts on the table, a swag bag filled with champagne and caviar, expensive bath products and lingerie. A heart-shaped pendant from Tiffany, a gold-plated pen for writing love notes." Kinga informed him.

Love notes? Did anyone send those anymore?

"Vouchers for romantic getaways, handwoven cashmere rugs, designer scarves and bags."

Wow, pricey. "Kind of like the swag bags they give away to the Oscar nominees?"

Kinga nodded. "The same firm who does those are doing ours, but because there are so many more people at our gala, they are just a smidgeon—" Kinga left a small space between her thumb and index finger "—cheaper. And I'm not exaggerating, our swag bag sponsors want our guests to use and purchase their products and are willing to donate accordingly. One Instagram post, one tweet and they've recouped their initial investment. You know how it works."

He did. He'd been paid big money to endorse products and the companies were always happy with the bump in sales.

"I read somewhere that the profits from the ball are donated to charity?" Griff said, enjoying their suddenly noncontentious conversation. Despite her saying that she didn't have any musical talent, her voice was melodic, a little edgy, like an expertly played saxophone piercing the late-night silence.

"We have sponsors but there are huge costs, obviously. Food, drink and talent being the top three most expensive items." Her amazing eyes pinned him to the sofa. "You are exorbitantly expensive, O'Hare."

Griff didn't bother to tell her that he'd quoted Ryder International a lower hourly rate than he normally charged because the profits from the event were going to charity. And if she was trying to make him feel bad about his remuneration, she was going to have to wait a while. He'd worked his ass off for more than twenty-five years to command the prices he did.

"We're hoping to raise around a hundred million for our foundation. My mom is the family representative on the foundation's board and that's her goal."

That was seriously impressive. He wasn't a slouch at donating. He quietly funneled considerable amounts to causes he believed in—fighting climate change and promoting literacy were two of his favorites—but this was next-level philanthropy. It inspired him to up his game.

Kinga leaned forward to put her wineglass on the coffee table, creating a gap between her pajama top and her chest and giving Griff a view of small but beautiful breasts.

God, he wanted her.

Kinga looked down at her clasped hands. "The Ryder name is associated with luxury and class and elegance. Our drinking establishments can be found in some of the most expensive and exclusive hotels all over the world. We host a ball for charity every year but this one, because it's our centenary year, has been designed to be our biggest and best one ever. It's a big deal.

"That's why I've been so vociferous about your involvement. I can't help but be scared that you will ruin our hard work and our reputation by doing something stupid, O'Hare."

He'd been called selfish and irresponsible, out of control and inconsiderate, and he'd trained himself to let the insults roll off his back. But her words, quietly uttered, hurt a lot more than they should.

Would she understand his reasoning for doing what he did? Would she understand his need to protect his twin? And weren't those stupid questions to ask himself, because he couldn't tell her or anyone else the truth?

"I will not tolerate you, or anyone else, derailing my event," Kinga added.

Griff looked at her pugnacious expression and sighed. "Would you believe me if I told you that I have no intention of doing anything of the sort?"

Kinga held his eyes and for half a heartbeat, Griff thought she might say that she did. Then her eyes cooled and she shook her head. "I believe you'd try, but you're impulsive and headstrong and I don't think you consider the consequences of your actions so, no, I wouldn't believe you."

He'd known that his past would come back to bite him in the ass and here it was, merrily snacking away.

Kinga picked up her wineglass and drained it, her

eyes not leaving his face. "So, where are you staying while you are in Portland?"

He was grateful for the change in subject. "I booked the Portland Harbor Hotel."

"I know it well. And are you going to stay there until the ball? You'll be inundated by the press and you won't have a moment's peace," Kinga pointed out.

Situation normal, Griff thought.

Kinga scrunched up her nose. "But I suppose that's a given wherever you are."

Unfortunately.

"So, are you going to be sticking around until the second week in February?" she asked, a little wistfully, suggesting that she already knew the answer to the question she'd asked him weeks before.

"I'm leaving tomorrow, after our meeting."

He needed to get back to his stud farm in Kentucky. Eloise was scheduled to take a four-day break and he needed to be around for Sam. Sian was a good mom, she loved her son but her condition required an extra set of hands and eyes. Nevertheless, spending time with Sam, and his sister, was one of his favorite things to do.

"But I need you to be in Portland until the concert."

Right, he could tolerate her bossiness—it amused him and he never allowed anyone to push him where he didn't want to go—but now she was being imperious. "Nope."

"What?"

Griff smiled at her. "Oh, sorry, that didn't come out right. No can do, *princess*."

He silently admitted that temporarily relocating to Portland did make sense. He should be on hand to give input into Kinga's decisions around his publicity and his favorite band members would be a lot more amenable to relocating to Portland than to his stud farm for practice sessions. But Sam and Sian came first and he couldn't leave Eloise with them on her own for weeks at a time.

Griff watched, amused, as annoyance filtered across Kinga's face and settled in her eyes. "If you are going to perform at *my* ball, I need you to be close at hand."

"No, you want to keep me out of trouble." Griff stood up abruptly and walked around the coffee table to place one hand on the arm of her sofa, bending down to look into her lovely face.

Kinga didn't bother to deny his words and Griff appreciated her honesty. She lifted her chin to stare at him, raising her arched eyebrows. She was trying so hard not to show any reaction, or her attraction, but Griff had enough experience with women—probably too much—and noticed her flushed skin and the erect nipples pushing against her pajama top. There were more subtle hints, too: her eyes had turned richer and darker, warmer, and she swallowed a few times, as if looking for moisture in her mouth. Her nails also burrowed into the thick material covering her couch and she sucked in a couple of harsh breaths.

But she never, not once, dropped her eyes from his. Stubborn, gorgeous woman.

"Or maybe you just want me close because you're ridiculously attracted to me," Griff murmured, his eyes dropping to her sexy, wide mouth.

"Dream on."

"Shall we put that notion to the test and see who is right?" Griff asked her, lowering his head so that his lips hovered over hers.

"I—"

Griff searched her face to make sure he wasn't reading her wrong—he never forced himself on anyone, ever—but before he could cover her lips with his, Kinga surprised him by grabbing a handful of his sweater and pulling him down. She arched her back and their mouths connected and...

Boom! Magic happened and his world imploded. All those crazy clichés he usually disdained suddenly made sense.

Yeah, this.

Judging by the way her tongue slid into his mouth, she was very into him. Maybe just as much as he was into her.

Damn, he was about to make this very complicated indeed, but he couldn't help himself. He'd been dreaming about doing this for what felt like a lifetime. But complicated was for later. Right now he wanted to take however much Kinga was offering.

Placing his knee on the cushion next to hers, Griff gripped the back of her head and tipped her head up to an angle he preferred. His lips danced along hers and he allowed his tongue to trace the seam of her mouth, coaxing her to open up, to let him in. At the same time, Kinga's hands moved from his clothing to his shoulders, she released a breath and her lips parted beneath his. Testing her response, needing to know if she was on board with where this was going, he pushed his tongue into the tiny gap, waiting for her reaction. Kinga, because she kept surprising him, widened her lips and her tongue tangled with his, as desperate to explore him as he was to discover her.

She was delightful, saucy and spicy, fierce and feisty, and he could kiss her for hours, days. Needing more, Griff hiked up her top, needing to feel her smooth skin under his broad hand. Smooth, soft, fragrant, gorgeous. His fingertips skimmed over her ribs and she released a tiny laugh into his mouth and Griff realized she was ticklish. Keeping his touch firm, he explored her tiny waist, her flat stomach and, leaving her skin, ran his hand down her hip, over her flannel-covered butt.

He fought the urge to pull her top over her head, to taste what he knew would be lovely nipples, to discover the honey between her legs. But, remembering her locks and her sister's concern, he wouldn't push. She'd only granted him permission to kiss her; the next move would be all hers.

As if hearing his thoughts, Kinga stiffened and pulled her mouth off his, pushing her hands against his chest to give her some space between them. Too much space…

But because he was a gentleman, even though few people knew it, Griff bounded to his feet and jammed his hands into the back pockets of his pants. He was sporting a massive erection but figured Kinga was an adult and should know that it was a natural outcome of a scorching hot kiss.

And yeah, thanks to his two-year-plus break from sex, he was rock-hard. And desperate to play. But Kinga's tense face was one big stop sign and he was backing off.

Kinga wrapped her arms around her bent knees and looked up at him with those wide, intense brown eyes. With her just-had-the-hell-kissed-out-of-her lips and flushed cheeks she looked stunning...

Man, he wanted her.

Almost as much as he didn't *want* to want her.

Griff rocked on his heels and looked around the room, wanting something to distract him from the gorgeous woman with her witchy eyes, to make him fight the urge to kiss her again.

The heavy silver photo frame facing the wall caught his eye again and he frowned at his surge of curiosity. Why have a photo if you weren't going to look at it? Who inspired such deep feelings in her that she couldn't bear to look at their image?

Why was he so fascinated by everything to do with her?

Right, he should go, right *now*. This was getting out of control.

But they hadn't touched on business yet.

"Would you like to join me for breakfast tomorrow at the hotel?" he asked. "Around eight?"

Griff saw that Kinga was still trying to get her brain into gear. Then the fogginess in her eyes cleared and she shook her head. "You'll be mobbed and we won't be able to finish a sentence. No, come to my office. I'll send you the directions—" she narrowed her eyes at him "—if you promise you'll read the damn text."

"I read every text you sent, sweetheart. I just stopped responding when you started repeating yourself."

"You didn't respond to any of my most recent ones!"

Griff winced. Hadn't he? He'd meant to, but he'd had his hands full with a colicky mare, a distracted Sian and a rambunctious Sam. The little spare time he'd had, he'd worked on choosing and testing his set list for the ball.

Not wanting to get into another argument, he dropped a kiss on her nose. "Get some sleep, sweetheart. I'll see you in the morning."

"Don't be late. I have a full day and can't wait around for you."

Kinga rubbed her forehead with her fingertips in a gesture Griff was coming to realize displayed her anxiety. He sent her what he hoped was a reassuring smile. "Relax, Kinga, it's all good."

Kinga's huge eyes flew up to collide with his. Color receded from her face and she seemed to shrink in on herself. "Don't say that!"

*It's all good?*

Why on earth would she object to that? But it was obvious the phrase disturbed her because he heard the pain in her voice, saw it in her eyes.

"I'm sorry?"

Kinga waved his apology away and stood up, wrapping her arms around her waist. "Ignore me, I'm just tired and it's been a very long day."

Yeah, he didn't buy that for a second. Knowing he couldn't push her, Griff started to walk away. He took two steps before stopping. After a short, internal debate around whether to vocalize his thoughts, he spoke. "I know you don't trust me, Kinga, but I won't let you down, I promise."

She didn't know it, but he seldom made promises, and the ones he did make, he always kept.

When he pulled back to look at her, her eyes reflected her skepticism and Griff realized it was going to take more than a sentence or two to get her to believe him.

And he was shocked at how much he wanted her to have faith in him.

# Four

Griff looked at himself in the reflective surface of the elevator and picked a piece of lint off his camel-colored jacket. In an effort to be taken seriously by the oh-so-stern Kinga, he'd worn dark blue jeans and a cream cable-knit sweater under the jacket.

He felt overdressed and a little stupid.

Good clothes wouldn't make her trust him... Or trust that he was the performer she was looking for, Griff amended. Despite their fiery kiss last night, a business relationship was the only type of relationship he could have with her. She wasn't, he knew, the type to have one-night stands or flings and he wasn't looking for anything permanent or complicated.

He had, so they said, baggage. A high-stress job, a bad reputation, a family with challenges.

He and Kinga were also, as he reminded himself, working together and her cooperation would ensure whether his comeback was a resounding success or a career-crushing failure.

There were more important things than her mouth under his, his hands on her spectacular body...

But because Griff was always brutally honest with himself, when he kissed her, or touched her, or even laid eyes on her, he tended to forget that salient point.

As much as he wanted to, he wouldn't misbehave today. Today he would show her that he could be professional. They'd talk about the publicity around the ball and how to manage the buzz his return would inevitably create.

He would not think about her spicy taste, her smooth skin...

The elevator doors opened and his phone vibrated. Stepping out, Griff pulled the phone from the inside pocket of his jacket and looked at the screen. He smiled, genuinely pleased to hear from his older half-sister.

Jan was born when his mother was seventeen and, because she was thirteen years older than him and Sian, and was already at college when he and Sian started in the industry, the press didn't know about her. She was his favorite secret, and she and her husband were among a handful of people who knew about Sian's condition and the lengths he'd gone to to protect her from the world.

"I'm about to go into a meeting, sweetheart. Can I call you when I'm done?"

"I'll make this quick," Jan assured him. She went on to explain that she, her husband and kids wanted to take Sam and Sian away with them for a few days and that Eloise would join them after her long weekend.

Jan's husband, Pete, an extremely wealthy, famous CEO, would hire a private jet to ensure their complete privacy.

"Where are you heading?" Griff asked, though he suspected he knew. Jan and Pete, with his blessing, had built a huge mansion on the opposite end of the island he'd purchased years ago, two nautical miles off Key Largo, completely overshadowing the modest bungalow he normally stayed in when he went down there.

It was their second home and they were spending more and more time in the Keys. Because they homeschooled their late-in-life kids, Griff suspected it would soon become their permanent abode. And that was fine by him.

"We might stay longer and Sam and Sian can stay as long as they like. You know how my girls adore having Sam around," Jan added. Jan's daughters, seven and five, considered Sam to be more of a baby brother than their cousin.

He trusted Jan and her levelheaded, down-to-earth husband to help Sian and Sam while Eloise was away. And Eloise would be happy to join them after her break. She loved the island.

And he could stay in Portland...

He told Jan to make the arrangements, told her

that he'd pick up the tab for the private jet and said goodbye, feeling a little guilty for feeling relieved that he didn't have to rush back to Kentucky. He'd been given some freedom, a little me-time, and he had no intention of wasting it.

It would give him a chance to, unhurriedly, work out the set list for the ball, to start practicing, to meet with the musicians he wanted for his band.

And to get to know Portland's Prickliest Princess a little better...

He bolted out from behind a pillar in the parking lot, scaring the hell out of her.

Kinga, in the process of opening her car door, let out a small scream and slapped her hand against her chest, gathering every bit of courage she had to face Mick Pritchard.

"Mick," she said, leaning back against her car, hoping he didn't realize that her legs were shaking and that she was terrified.

*You are not eighteen anymore, Kinga, and he wouldn't dare punch you again.* Not here, in the Ryder International garage, with cameras everywhere.

"What are you doing here?"

"I thought we needed to chat."

"I thought vicious emails and text messages were more your style," Kinga snapped, her anger chasing away a little of her fear.

Mick slid his hands into the pockets of his expensive coat. He was doing very well for himself. His coat was cashmere, his shoes were designer, as was his suit. But Kinga wasn't impressed and she'd lost all respect for the boy she'd grown up with when he'd backhanded her after Jas's funeral. For that, she'd never forgiven him.

He'd not only blamed her for Jas's death but, by assaulting her, he'd taken away her trust in men, in people generally.

"I wanted to tell you that I am entering politics. I am going to run for mayor of Portland. I plan to run on a law-and-order ticket, making our town safe again type of thing. I have a big press conference announcing the news next month."

Kinga's heart sank. Jesus. Why was life punishing her?

"And you're asking my permission?" Kinga sarcastically asked, knowing her statement was the exact opposite of the truth.

Mick snorted. "As if. No, I want you to get me an audience with Jas's father so that I can explain my intentions. He's not taking my calls and he won't meet with me."

Mick had to be desperate if he was reaching out to her. Kinga narrowed her eyes and crossed her arms over her chest. "That could be because you've used his daughter's death in your company's promotional videos. Why do you want to see him?"

When he didn't answer, a thought crossed Kinga's mind. Her mouth dropped open. "Oh my God, you want him to endorse you!"

Mick didn't look even remotely embarrassed. He simply shrugged. "It's politics, Kinga."

"It's *sick*, Mick! You've spent years capitalizing on her tragic death and you want her father to simply forget that? You son of a bitch!" Kinga shouted, furious beyond belief. "No, I will not pass on your message, but I will warn him about you. Maybe Seth will campaign against you."

Mick's strong hand shot out to grip her forearm and his fingertips dug into her skin. "Be very careful, Kinga."

Kinga, refusing to show her terror, jerked her arm from his grip. "Don't you ever lay hands on me again, Pritchard! I am not that sad, young girl I once was!"

His eyes narrowed and his expression darkened. She recognized that look—she'd seen it before, seconds before he struck her.

"Everything that happens in this garage is filmed and recorded, Pritchard, and if you hit me again, this time I won't hesitate to press charges."

His fist bunched tighter and Kinga held her breath, knowing he was fighting for control, but after a minute, maybe more, his hand relaxed.

"Leave me, and the Garwoods, alone, Mick."

"I stopped listening to you the moment I realized it was your fault Jas died," Mick coldly informed her.

There was no point in arguing. It was, after all, the truth.

Knowing she was either going to cry or collapse, Kinga abruptly turned and yanked open the door to her car, sliding into her seat and immediately locking her doors. She hit the start button, slapped the car into Reverse and watched Mick in her rearview mirror as she sped out of the garage.

A half hour later, exhausted and emotional, Kinga pulled her car into one of the three parking spaces outside her home and cursed the weather. She'd yet again left her umbrella at work. Hard raindrops, containing flecks of snow, hit her windshield. She considered the distance between her car and the front door and wondered whether she had the energy to make it to her door.

She was that tired.

She'd fought off a panic attack since leaving the parking garage, and now that she was finally home, she could feel its cold fingers dancing up her throat, squeezing. She knew she was safe, that Mick wouldn't hurt her again but, despite a decade passing, she could still hear the awful sound of his hand connecting with her cheekbone, see the fury on his face. The spittle in the corner of his mouth, the anger in his eyes...

*"You stupid bitch! You let her die. She was my everything! I had plans, dammit!"*

Kinga leaned her forehead on the steering wheel, her heart rate inching upward. Lifting her hand, her fingers bounced up and down and her throat tightened. It was after eight and she didn't need to experience a panic attack in her car on one of the coldest evenings of the year.

Her first goal was to get inside, but her front

door was a hundred miles away. She was short of breath and incapable of movement. Getting there seemed an impossible task. She knew she had to move, but the feeling of impending doom, of sheer terror, wouldn't allow her to open the door or climb out of her car.

Kinga turned her head and looked at her cell phone lying on the passenger seat next to her. She brushed her finger over the screen and saw that her last call was to O'Hare fifteen minutes ago… She'd asked something about the press conference they'd scheduled for tomorrow to formally announce his comeback but couldn't remember what.

Her memory was always spotty when she felt like she was dying. But she did know Tinsley and their best friend, Jules, were out of town and her parents would take more than a half hour to reach her.

She needed someone right now and, somehow and strangely, it felt right for her to call Griff.

He answered almost immediately. "Will you please stop fussing, princess? I've done a million press conferences before."

Kinga swallowed, tried to speak and swallowed again.

"Kinga?" His voice sharpened and she could easily imagine him sitting up, his eyes narrowing. "What's wrong?"

"Can you come?" she asked, her voice thready. "To my apartment?"

"On my way," Griff instantly responded. "Do you need help? Should I call 911?"

"No. I'm fine." Sort of. "I just need some help." *Getting to my front door.*

When he got here, he'd realize she wasn't the strong, always-in-control woman he thought she was. Kinga cursed herself for her impulsive decision to call him. What the hell had she been thinking? He was a business associate, not a friend.

"Look, don't worry, I'm fine. I'll make a plan."

But looking into the dark, she didn't know if she could. Jas had died in the dark, a short distance from her home. Kinga's head swam...

"Shut up," Griff ordered, his tone harsh. "I'm coming."

The minutes—hours, years—passed and Kinga held the steering wheel in a death grip, finding it increasingly difficult to get air into her lungs, feeling like the car was closing in on her. A short, sharp rap on her door made her jump and she turned to see an indistinct blob standing outside her car. She screamed and fumbled for the button to check whether she'd locked the car, forgetting that she always, always locked her car.

"Dammit, Kinga, it's me, Griff!"

She looked at him through the rain-wet window and it took a minute, maybe more, to recognize his face, hair plastered against his head, his dark green eyes worried and his normally sensual mouth stern.

Griff tapped on the window. "Open the goddamn door, Kinga."

Kinga hit the locks and Griff pulled the door open, and the shock of cold air had her gasping.

The sound of her seat belt releasing sounded like a gunshot and then she felt two warm hands on her face. She stared into Griff's eyes, wishing she could breathe.

"What's wrong with you?"

She just managed to whisper the words. "Panic attack."

"Right, I want you to breathe with me. In for four, hold it..." Kinga listened to the command in his voice, his eyes a lifeline in a topsy-turvy world. "Now blow out in a steady stream. I'm here, sweetheart, I've got you. Right now, all I want you to do is breathe in and out," Griff told her, his gaze warm and sympathetic and his voice oh-so-steady.

"You've stopped taking deep breaths, honey. Come on now. In for four, hold it and release in a long, steady stream."

Kinga concentrated on his words and closed her eyes, sucking in air. She held her breath before releasing it in as long a stream as she could. It took three or four, maybe more, times before she felt her heart rate dropping and her tight chest easing. Kinga placed her hand on Griff's shoulder and she felt his warmth through his leather jacket and the ice in her veins started to dissolve...

A few more minutes passed and eventually, she felt the last tendrils of fear flee, felt like she could breathe properly. As oxygen hit her brain, Kinga started to take in some details. His car was parked in Tinsley's space, the door open and the light on, and it looked like he'd barreled out of the vehicle without locking up, as if he'd rushed to get to her.

He sat on his haunches outside of her car, snow falling on his bare head, but his eyes fixed on her, his expression sympathetic.

"You okay now? Chest and throat loose?"

Kinga nodded. "Yeah." She shivered, feeling the wind whipping around her legs and rustling her short hair. "God, you must be freezing," she stated.

Griff shrugged and stood up. "I've been warmer. Let's get you inside, sweetheart."

The endearment sounded good on his lips, like it belonged there. Kinga looked at the strong, tan hand he held out to her and placed her palm in his, allowing him to help her out of the car. Knowing that her knees tended to be a bit liquid after a panic attack, she held on, not wanting to fall facedown onto the snow-covered pavement.

Debilitating tiredness would soon follow and she hoped to be in her apartment before it struck.

Griff ducked into her car and picked up her bag, snagging her car keys from the ignition. He slammed the car door closed.

"I'll come back and sort out my car and get your laptop," Griff told her, wrapping his arm around her waist. "Have you got your keys?"

"In my coat pocket." She leaned into him, happy for his support, and let out a squeal when he picked her up and cradled her against his broad chest. "Griff, I can walk."

"I'm sure you can, but I'm freezing and would

like to get inside before I turn into an icicle." Griff strode across the small patch of lawn and hurried up the steps leading to the front door of her building. He asked her for her code, punched it in on the keypad and used his shoulder to push the door open. Two paces later he was at the door to her apartment and, balancing her on his upraised knee—God, the guy was strong—dug around in her coat pocket with his free hand to pull out her set of keys.

At her direction, he found the right key, turned the knob and walked into her home. Kinga inhaled the warm air and the subtle scent of fresh flowers and beeswax polish. This was her safe place, her sanctuary. She relaxed immediately. Nobody could hurt her here.

Exhaustion washed over her in a steady wave.

She glanced over to her still open door, tasted panic again—Mick's furious face popped up on the screen of her mind—and reminded herself that he wouldn't be foolish enough to follow her home, to push his case. Besides, right now she had her very own, very brawny bodyguard. Not wanting to lose this sense of security, she rested her head against Griff's wet chest and sighed. She'd take being wet above being scared any day of the week.

Kinga felt his lips in her hair before he loosened his grip on her and allowed her feet to drop to the floor. He gently lowered her to sit on the closest sofa and dropped to his haunches again, concerned. "Better? Want some tea or something?"

He ran his hand around the back of his neck and

Kinga realized that he was wetter and colder than she'd thought. His jeans were dark with rain, his hair was slicked back and his lips held a tinge of blue. "You should get out of those wet clothes," she suggested, her voice still weak.

His lips quirked. "Are you trying to get me naked, sweetheart?"

His teasing made her smile. "I'm trying to ensure that you don't get hypothermia, O'Hare."

Kinga yawned and she covered her mouth with her hand. Then she yawned again.

"Exhaustion often follows an extreme panic attack. Let's get you to bed."

Kinga wanted to make a joke, say something witty and funny but couldn't muster the mental strength to think of anything. She just wanted to sleep. But the door was open and anyone could walk inside...

"Can you shut the door, hit the locks when you leave?" she asked, and cursed the tremor in her voice. Despite knowing how weak she sounded, she couldn't stop her next sentence. "Will you check, and check again, that I'm locked in?"

Griff's face hardened. "At some point, we're going to have a chat about what's got you so scared, Kinga." Then his expression lightened and Kinga noticed that his eyes were as warm as the hand cradling her cheek was cold. "Would you sleep better if I stayed here?"

She wanted to brush away his offer, tell him she was an independent woman, that she could take care of herself. But her actions tonight completely negated that statement, and she would sleep better knowing he was within shouting distance.

Why was she so comfortable with him?

"Kinga, do you want me to stay?"

She wanted to lie, to tell him to go, but she was too tired to make the effort. "Yes, please."

She'd deal with the consequences of her impulsive decision in the morning. Because, as she knew, every action had consequences.

The next morning, after a night spent in her spare bedroom, Griff used Kinga's espresso machine to deliver a much-needed hit of caffeine. Taking his cup back to the living room, he decided to satisfy his curiosity and picked up the heavy silver frame Kinga had turned to face the wall.

It was a perfectly normal photograph of Kinga—much younger, with long, braided hair—and a dark-eyed, dark-haired girl, both beaming at the camera. They wore beanies and huge smiles, and there was nothing in the photograph to explain why she couldn't look at it.

He was now more curious than he'd been before. Not good.

Griff heard footsteps on the stairs, replaced the photograph and walked over to the window to pull back the drapes. The weather was continuing its dismal streak. The rain and snow had stopped but the clouds were low in the sky, as if deciding whether to dump more moisture on the already soaked land.

"Morning."

Griff turned to look at Kinga, dressed in black jeans and a black cashmere sweater under a black-and-white houndstooth jacket. Trendy black-and-white sneakers covered her feet. He sighed at her don't-ask-me expression but was unable to get her pale, terrified face out of his mind. He was so used to Kinga's quick mouth and her in-your-face attitude, and seeing her vulnerability last night had shaken him.

What in God's name could've happened to cause his alpha boss girl to have a panic attack? Not for the first, or fiftieth, time he wondered what Kinga was hiding behind her I-can-do-anything-and-be-anything facade?

"You're looking better," Griff told her.

Kinga sent him a wry smile. "I could hardly look any worse."

Griff watched as she made herself coffee, waiting for an explanation he knew wouldn't come. He leaned against the state-of-the-art gas cooker, crossing his legs at the ankles.

After giving her a minute or two to get some caffeine into her system, he spoke again.

"Do you get panic attacks often?"

Her eyes collided with his, and he smiled at the soft expletive she didn't mean for him to hear. Ah, so she'd been intending to fudge her way out of the experience, obviously hoping she could spin a BS story.

"Ah, I—" Kinga pushed her hand through her hair, making the short ends stand up on one side. It was a cute look on her. She wrinkled her nose and when her shoulders slumped, Griff knew she'd given up on the idea of finding a fake explanation for what had happened. "I haven't had one for a few years, thank God." She sipped her coffee, wrapping both hands around the mug.

"What triggers them? Is it a specific event or general anxiety?"

His first memory of Sian having a panic attack was when they were eight and about to do a live segment for a Christmas special. She'd passed out and the producers had rearranged the lineup to put them later in the program. Someone, possibly Finn, had given her something to calm her, and Sian was able to sing.

Looking back, he cursed both Finn and their parents for pushing them so hard to constantly perform. He'd been able to cope with the pressure but Sian, who was by far the better musician, vocalist and performer, didn't enjoy the limelight. Her biggest dream growing up was to be a normal kid doing normal things.

Griff raised one eyebrow, silently reminding Kinga that she hadn't answered his question about what triggered her panic attacks. Kinga ignored his silent demand and changed the subject. "We need to get moving. Your press conference is in an hour and you still need to change. And shave."

He rubbed his hand over his not-too-heavy stubble.

"And please wear something nice."

Yep, the princess was back. Griff was both sad

and relieved. And while a pair of old jeans and a T-shirt sounded great—clothes he felt incredibly comfortable in—he had planned to wear something similar to what he'd worn yesterday, business boring.

It was his first press conference in years and, annoyingly, it would help if he made a good impression.

"Are you nervous?" Kinga asked him, her lovely eyes meeting his. He didn't do morning-after conversations, but he had no problem with Kinga being the first thing he looked at in the morning. He rather liked her face...

And her body.

Recalling her question, he shrugged. He wasn't, not particularly. And especially not if he compared it to the flat-out terror he'd felt when he heard Kinga asking him for help.

And, as he said, he'd done what seemed like a million press conferences before.

But none of them had been this important...

He was, officially, about to launch his comeback and he needed this morning to go well. Or as well as it could. It was going to be a helluva story and, since it was *his* life and *his* career, Griff figured he was facing a barrage of ugly questions.

Luckily, with Sian being in the Keys, she'd be far away from any reporter wanting to get his sister's reaction to his comeback plans. As per normal, they wouldn't find her. The island's ownership was hidden behind a couple of LLCs and they wouldn't trace her through Jan, who had a different maiden name and married surname than them. Jan was also married to a reclusive Fortune 500 CEO who took his privacy very, very seriously.

Sian and Sam would not be caught up in the press hype. And that was all he cared about.

"They are going to ask a lot of rude and intrusive questions. Don't answer them, just move on," Kinga told him, her expression worried. She glanced at her watch. "We have fifteen minutes or so before we need to leave, so we can do a dry run."

"A what?" he asked, heading back to the coffee machine. He needed, he estimated, a gallon more to feel human.

"Why did you divorce your first wife four months after you married her?" The question was like a bullet, but he saw the curiosity in her eyes.

"Because I was twenty-one and thought I was in love. Greta didn't love me, she just needed to marry to extend her working visa and I was a means to that goal," Griff told her, surprising himself by giving her the unsanitized version.

She had a way of pulling the truth out of him.

"Wrong answer. Rather tell them that you refuse to discuss your private life," Kinga informed him.

"I wasn't answering them, I was satisfying your curiosity," he remarked, before turning back to the machine.

"I'm not curious."

Griff finished making his coffee, and when he faced her again, he raised both his brows, watching as her cheeks colored. The hell she wasn't curious...

"So she got her visa extended and filed for a divorce?"

Griff lifted his cup to hide his smile. "Pretty much."

His ex was now one of the highest-paid actresses in the business, happily married, and hated, as much as he did, any references to their super-brief wedding. He'd forgiven her a long time ago, knowing that his ego and pride had taken a hit but not his heart.

Kinga pulled in a deep breath. Picking up a teaspoon, she held it to her mouth, mimicking holding a microphone. "Has Stan Maxwell forgiven you and Ava? Do you regret kissing your best friend's wife in that New York nightclub?"

Like the rest of the world, Kinga believed his and Ava's excellent acting. If there was one story he deeply regretted manufacturing, the Manhattan club episode would be top of his list. It had all happened so fast, triggered by a reporter who'd continuously hassled his then-publicist for a response to allegations that Sian was both depressed and pregnant.

They needed a massive story to counteract the one the reporter was planning on publishing and, desperate, Griff had sought Stan and Ava's advice. Trusting his two best friends implicitly, he'd explained that his bad boy routine was just a ruse and that Sian was, indeed, suffering from serious mental health issues. And that she was three months pregnant.

They'd immediately asked how they could help, and it was Ava who suggested they anonymously tip off the reporter, that he be the one to catch them cuddling. Ava and Stan's relationship was fantastically secure, and as one of the world's golden couples, they could withstand gossip. The reporter got the scoop, Sian was ignored and Griff became, in the eyes of the world, a class A prick.

He desperately wanted to explain to Kinga that he wasn't the disloyal, marriage-wrecking bastard the press portrayed him to be.

But he couldn't. Nobody could know...

"Back off, darlin'," he quietly suggested.

Kinga snorted, not at all intimidated. "They are going to ask."

In his previous life, when he spoke in that tone of voice, people—including his ex-manager— immediately backed down. Not Kinga. And he liked that about her. He just didn't like her nosiness.

"I can deal with the press." He saw that she was about to argue, and spoke before she could. "Have I pressed you about your panic attacks? Demanded to know who is the dark-haired girl in the silver frame? Asked why you can't bear to look at her?"

Kinga wrinkled her nose, something she tended to do, he realized, when she didn't have an immediate answer or solution.

She sat down and slumped back in her chair. "Fair point. I just don't want you to be caught flat-footed this morning."

Griff hid his smile. It was a decent excuse and he admired her quick mind. But, bored with the inter-rogation—he was about to do this again in a couple of hours—Griff decided to give her something else to take her mind off business.

And her panic attack.

Walking around the kitchen island, he gathered the material of her thin sweater in his fingers. Wrapping it in his fist, he gently pulled the fabric, silently asking her to stand up. Once on her feet, she inched closer. She might not want to work with him, but she was attracted to him.

As he was to her…

"What are you doing?" Kinga asked as he closed the gap between her mouth and his.

"I'm tired of arguing with you and I'd much rather do this. Wouldn't you?"

When she nodded, he kept his kiss gossamer soft, giving her the choice to take their kiss deeper or not. Only she would know whether she wanted hard and intense or light and lingering, so he didn't push. Kinga placed her hands on his chest and tipped her head to the side, her body taut. He traced the seam of her lips with his tongue, and on a puff of sweet air, her lips parted and invited him to take the kiss deeper.

Pulling her into him, Griff wrapped his arms around her and felt her body liquefy, her tension dissolve. It would be so easy to light that fuse—to take their kiss deeper, to fall into passion—but Griff knew that wasn't what either of them needed.

Sometime in the future, God willing, he'd have her naked and panting, but not this morning. Beneath her prickles and her snark, she was tired and vulnerable and no man with any honor took advantage of that.

And despite what the world thought, honor was still important to him.

Griff eased back with great reluctance, his mouth lifted from hers, and his thumb slid against her bottom lip.

"Let's get moving, Kinga. And we'll pick up this discussion later."

Kinga stepped back and smoothed down her sweater. When her eyes met his, they were, once again, filled with annoyed determination. "We most certainly will. For the record, I don't like your high-handed manner of changing the subject, O'Hare."

Griff smiled at her. "And just for the record, I still want to know why you have panic attacks."

Her mouth opened and snapped closed, and when she remained silent, Griff thought he just might have won this round.

But with someone as intriguing, enigmatic and plain sexy as Kinga, who the hell knew.

# Five

Right, well…

That went as well as she'd expected it to.

In the small meeting room adjacent to the conference room where they'd held the press conference to announce Griff's comeback, Kinga sank into a chair, put her elbows on her thighs and stared at the carpet below her feet. She felt like she'd gone ten rounds with a sumo wrestler.

Sitting next to Griff, she'd been asked a few questions about the ball, and how far Ryder International had come in a century, but most of the questions, and *all* of the interest, had been directed at Griff. The room had been fascinated with his return to the limelight.

And despite her telling the press that his private

life was off-limits, he'd been bombarded with questions about his past.

*"Why did you divorce Greta after four months?"*

*"Have you racked up anymore DUIs?"*

*"Stan Maxwell threatened to sue you when pictures of you and his wife kissing in a corner of a notorious New York nightclub were leaked to the press. Did you settle out of court and how much did you have to pay your former best friend?"*

*"Who is your current girlfriend, Griff? And have you cheated on her yet?"*

*"Is Sian thinking about making a comeback as well? Where is she? Why haven't we seen her for years?"*

The rude, intrusive questions were machine-gun fast and had Kinga feeling weirdly protective, a stupid reaction because Griff was the last person in the world who needed or wanted her protection. Throughout the torture session, she'd worked damn hard to keep her expression bland.

Griff, to his credit, had handled the press with aplomb and good humor. He ignored the rude reporters, repeatedly telling the big crowd that he'd only answer questions about his comeback, his upcoming performance at the Ryder ball, and his future career plans.

They'd persisted, but Griff just handed the offenders hard stares and took the next question. After an hour of watching the reporters pummel Griff, Kinga had called the press conference to an end.

If she felt like she needed a shot of tequila before

lying down, then Griff had to feel like he'd been run over by a tank.

Frankly, it had been a brutal twenty-four hours. She always felt drained after a panic attack and she'd had to spend extra time on her makeup earlier to cover the dark stripes under her eyes. Her thoughts kept bouncing from wondering whether Mick would ever leave her be—she'd received another text message from him this morning demanding another meeting—to how sweet Griff had been when she'd called him the night before.

Griff was, reputedly, everything she didn't need in her life: a hard-living bad boy and a self-absorbed celebrity. But she'd still called him. He'd arrived quickly, provided his strength and support and had, to her surprise, stuck around. And, as he'd pointed out, he hadn't peppered her with questions. He'd respected her privacy.

She hadn't respected his.

In her defense, she desperately wanted to understand what drove him, what motivated him, why he acted like an entitled, spoiled superstar.

Because Kinga was starting to suspect that he wasn't as bad as he was reported to be.

She had no evidence to back up her suspicions, but she had a gut-deep feeling that she, and the rest of the world, were missing some crucial information.

The door opened behind her and Kinga turned to see a relaxed-looking Griff walk into the room, followed by...*holy shit*, Stan Maxwell, the front man of one of the world's most famous rock groups, Milestone. His wife, the ex-supermodel turned actress Ava Brandon, was at his side. Ava wore tight, ripped-at-the-knee jeans, Doc Martens boots and a twenty-thousand-dollar designer jacket.

Stan, as was his habit, wore black. Black jeans, black V-neck sweater, black high-tops.

Kinga slowly stood up, her eyes darting from Griff to Stan to Ava and back to Griff. Why were they all here, together? Weren't they supposed to hate each other? Her brain struggled to make sense of their obvious affection for each other as Stan had his hand on Griff's shoulder and Ava's smile reflected both worry and concern.

They were unaware she was in the room. And as Kinga watched, Griff pulled Ava into a hug, wrapping his arm around the model's waist and holding her head against his shoulder. "I can't believe you guys are here. Jesus, this is an unexpected treat, but please, for the love of God, promise me nobody knows you are here."

"We've gotten good at fooling the paparazzi," Stan replied. "We used the back entrance and the staff corridors. We watched the press conference in the limo."

"But what are you doing here?" Griff asked, as Ava stepped away from him to take her husband's hand.

"You didn't think we were going to let you face that rabble for the first time without us being here, if only in the background, giving you moral support, right?" Ava asked, a hand on her slim hip.

Kinga stared at them, trying to wrap her head around the fact that the participants in Griff's most notorious scandal were in Portland, in this room.

"We put out a fake story that we're going to our cabin in Vail so anyone looking for us will look for us there. But honestly, since our wedding and you falling off the face of the earth, the press attention has lessened considerably," Stan stated.

"Thank you for being here," Griff said. "I can't tell you how grateful I am, and how much I appreciate all that you've done—"

"Hi! You must be Kinga," Ava loudly stated, cutting off Griff's words. Kinga couldn't decide if Ava was being rude or if she was trying to stop Griff from continuing his sentence.

Griff whirled around and his eyes widened on seeing her. She saw a hint of panic in his deep green gaze before his expression slid into impassivity. "I thought you'd left, Kinga," Griff said, rubbing the back of his neck. "You said you were heading back to your office."

"I thought I'd take a minute to decompress and this room was handy," Kinga explained. She sent Ava and Stan a quick smile. "I'm Kinga Ryder-White. I handle Ryder International's PR and publicity."

Stan held out his hand to shake Kinga's and introduced his wife. Kinga suppressed her burning questions. Why they were still friends if Griff kissed Stan's wife in a New York nightclub and was then photographed leaving her apartment the next morning? Stan had threatened to sue Griff. Was this some weird ménage à trois? Why did Kinga feel she was missing something big?

She tried to act normal. Well, as normal as one could act when in the presence of two incredibly famous musicians and an actress/model who was as well-known for her climate change activism as she was for her lovely face and gorgeous body.

Griff gestured for them all to sit. "I appreciate you being here," he told his friends, sitting next to Kinga on the two-seater couch, his thigh pressing into hers. "How do you think the press conference went?"

Ava looked at Stan before speaking. "The news that you are returning to work is explosive and everyone will run the story. But with the good comes the bad, and they will dredge up the past."

Kinga turned her head to look at Griff's profile, noticing that his jaw was tight with tension. "For what's it worth, I thought you were wonderful. You were completely professional, and you handled the questions with humor and class," she told him.

Griff smiled, his expression amused. "Thank you. I've been doing this for a long, long time, Kinga." Turning to his friends, he gestured to Kinga. "Kinga has spent the last week dreading this press conference. She was convinced that I'd lose my shit and embarrass her and Ryder International."

"I did not say that!" Kinga vehemently retorted. When Griff raised his eyebrows in protest, Kinga tossed her hands up in the air.

"You thought it," Griff said, and Kinga heard a note in his voice she couldn't identify. He couldn't be feeling hurt at her lack of faith, could he? No, she was letting her imagination run away from her.

Ava rested her forearms on her thighs and checked her watch. "The car will be here to collect us soon." She looked at Griff. "What are your plans today? Stan and I have meetings in Manhattan later, but we've been invited to Frodo's tonight. Geraint wants to test his new menu on us. We're sneaking in the back door and using the private dining room. Do you want to join us?"

Kinga had grown up wealthy and was used to a certain amount of local fame, but these people were in a league of their own. Frodo's was a multi-Michelin star restaurant in Manhattan and Geraint Du Pont was its lauded, avant-garde chef. Normal people were required to wait eighteen months and to take out a personal loan to eat his creations.

Griff looked at Kinga. "Well?"

Kinga frowned, surprised. "I'm invited?"

"Sure," Ava said, her expression friendly. "But we'd need to leave quite soon if we are to make our meetings. The Gulfstream is waiting at the airport."

Griff looked at her, waiting for her response. She was so tempted, but there was no way she could just blow off the rest of the day to take a jaunt with these superstars. She had a ball to organize and a to-do list as long as her arm to get through. "Uh, thank you, but I really can't."

Ava's smile reflected her disappointment. "Pity, I was looking forward to getting to know you better."

Why? Kinga ran her fingers across her forehead,

trying to make sense of what was happening. Griff had had an affair, a one-night stand, a *something* with his best friend's wife. Yet here they were, all acting like the paparazzi hadn't caught him with his mouth on hers or her hand on his butt. Maybe they'd all forgotten?

Ava looked at Griff and then smiled at her husband.

"She has that what-the-hell-is-happening look," she said, unfurling her long body and standing up. Stan followed her to his feet and immediately wrapped his arm around her waist, sending Kinga a sympathetic smile.

Kinga shrugged, following the others to her feet. "I admit, I'm a bit thrown by this dynamic."

Griff glared at his friends before looking at Kinga, his expression impassive. "I'm sorry you can't join us. I think you would've enjoyed Geraint's food."

She was sure she would've too.

"Bring me back a Lombardi's pizza and a slice of cheesecake from Junior's," Kinga joked.

"I'll see you tomorrow, sweetheart," Griff said.

God, her heart melted like an ice cube under a blowtorch every time he called her an endearment in his raspy, sexy voice. "Have fun," Kinga told him, unable to keep her eyes from darting to Stan's big hand on his wife's hip.

Ava stepped forward, took Kinga's hands and placed a kiss on her right cheek, then her left, before holding her own cheek against Kinga's to speak in her ear. "There's always a story under the story, honey. The truth is never simple and seldom found on entertainment websites."

Ava stepped back and smiled at her. "I hope we meet again." Turning to her husband, she held out her hand, which Stan took. "New York, baby?"

"Anywhere with you," Stan said, his smile soft and loving. "But honestly, I think Kinga's idea of Lombardi pizza and New York cheesecake is a far better idea than the bite-size concoctions Geraint serves."

"Monster," Ava told him.

Griff's fingers briefly hooked with Kinga's as he walked past her. "We'll catch up later," he told her.

Kinga nodded and crossed her arms over her jacket, wondering what the hell had just happened.

They weren't just missing something about Griff O'Hare. Kinga suspected they all might be missing *everything*.

That afternoon, Kinga attended a hastily convened meeting between the top management of Ryder International in Callum's private boardroom. They touched on quarterly returns and Ryder's expansion into China and Japan, but most of the attention— Callum's especially—was on the upcoming ball and the other celebrations to mark their hundred years in business.

Kinga was particularly excited about Tinsley's new project: a specialty cocktail competition. Ryder International bars, in the US and overseas, employed specialty mixologists to serve both mundane and unusual cocktails to their guests. The mixologists could enter either as a team or on their own, but they needed to create four new cocktails inspired by four different events over the last one hundred years. There would be regional, national and international winners.

At Tinsley and Kinga's request, Callum increased their centenary celebration budget by another twenty million, which was both surprising and helpful. Possibly because Griff's fee to sing at the ball was astronomical. Nobody else had a problem with Griff or was even remotely worried about him or his antics spoiling their launch event.

Even her anxiety about his performance was rapidly receding…

Now, thinking back on her intense, fast-paced day, Kinga sat on her sofa in her apartment and told herself, yet again, that it didn't matter whether her perception of Griff was changing. The world considered him a vain, self-absorbed bad boy and that was the image she had to work with.

And despite having more confidence in Griff, there was no getting away from the fact that he had failed to show up for performances a few times before.

What if he did that again?

She wanted to believe him when he said he wouldn't let her down but how could she? The best predictor of future behavior was past behavior, so…

She had to protect her event. She could not allow herself to become complacent.

# Treat Yourself with 2 Free Books!

Strictly Confidential
DONNA HILL

**Sizzling Romance**

HARLEQUIN PRESENTS
How to Tempt the Off-Limits Billionaire
JOSS WOOD

LARGER PRINT

**Passionate Romance**

# GET UP TO 4 FREE BOOKS & 2 FREE GIFTS WORTH OVER $20

## See Inside For Details

# Get ready to relax and indulge with your FREE BOOKS and more!

## Claim up to FOUR NEW BOOKS & TWO MYSTERY GIFTS – absolutely FREE!

Dear Reader,

We both know life can be difficult at times. That's why it's important to treat yourself so you can relax and recharge once in a while.

And I'd like to help you do this by sending you this amazing offer of up to FOUR brand new full length FREE BOOKS that WE pay for.

**This is everything I have ready to send to you right now:**

Try **Harlequin® Desire** books featuring the worlds of the American elite with juicy plot twists, delicious sensuality and intriguing scandal.

Try **Harlequin Presents® Larger-Print** books featuring the glamorous lives of royals and billionaires in a world of exotic locations, where passion knows no bounds.

Or **TRY BOTH!**

All we ask in return is that you answer 4 simple questions on the attached Treat Yourself survey. You'll get **Two Free Books** and **Two Mystery Gifts** from each series you try, *altogether worth over $20*! Who could pass up a deal like that?

Sincerely,

*Pam Powers*

Harlequin Reader Service

# Treat Yourself to Free Books and Free Gifts.

## Answer 4 fun questions and get rewarded.

◄ **DETACH AND MAIL CARD TODAY!** ►

| | YES | NO |
|---|---|---|
| 1. I LOVE reading a good book. | | |
| 2. I indulge and "treat" myself often. | | |
| 3. I love getting FREE things. | | |
| 4. Reading is one of my favorite activities. | | |

### TREAT YOURSELF • Pick your 2 Free Books...

Yes! Please send me my Free Books from each series I select and Free Mystery Gifts. I understand that I am under no obligation to buy anything, as explained on the back of this card.

Which do you prefer?

❏ **Harlequin Desire®** 225/326 HDL GRAN
❏ **Harlequin Presents® Larger-Print** 176/376 HDL GRAN
❏ **Try Both** 225/326 & 176/376 HDL GRAY

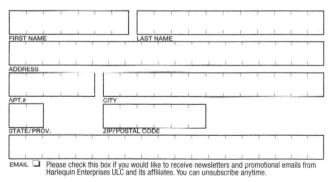

FIRST NAME          LAST NAME

ADDRESS

APT.#          CITY

STATE/PROV.          ZIP/POSTAL CODE

EMAIL ❏  Please check this box if you would like to receive newsletters and promotional emails from Harlequin Enterprises ULC and its affiliates. You can unsubscribe anytime.

HD/HP-520-TY22

And that meant having a backup plan.

If she had made a backup plan to get Jas home, her friend would still be alive.

Pushing away those dark thoughts, Kinga ran through a list of artists and entertainers she used regularly. As soon as she got Griff's set list, she'd hire a vocalist to be his understudy, ready to step in if anything went wrong.

And she wasn't just overplanning when it came to Griff; she had contingency plans for *everything*. She was splitting the catering between three different companies—so that if one had an issue, the others could step in. She'd hired more bartenders than necessary to ensure great service, knowing that if a few didn't show up to work, the guests' enjoyment wouldn't be compromised. She had a second florist on standby and, on a personal level, she had three ball gowns in case she spilled wine or food on herself.

This ball was being touted as one of the entertainment events of the decade—she would not allow anything or anyone to spoil it.

Kinga heard the beep of a message landing on her phone and quickly picked it up, relieved that it wasn't a voice mail from Mick again. He'd briefly and insincerely apologized for ambushing her in the parking garage and asked her, again, to intervene on his behalf with Senator Seth Garwood. He'd also, interestingly, asked whether she planned on disclosing his lack of control to the press—she presumed he meant revealing how he'd punched her. He reminded her that if she did, it would be a "he said, she said" situation.

No, she was keeping quiet about that. She didn't need any interest from the media that wasn't directly related to the ball. Besides, she'd never told anyone about Mick's lack of control. Tinsley and her parents would be hurt and furious if they found out.

No, no good would come of saying anything. But Mick didn't need to know that.

Other news of the day was that Callum still hadn't received the results of their family's DNA tests, and he was not happy. Her blue-blooded grandfather was obsessed with the Ryder-White family tree and their reputation as one of the state's first families. Kinga knew he was itching to discover other links to some of the area's, and America's, founding families.

Her father and mother, it had to be noted, were also surprisingly invested in the outcome. Why did they suddenly seem to care about DNA tests and who was related to whom?

God, she didn't know if she could cope if they started banging on about blood and the importance of the family tree. Callum's obsession with legacy was more than enough. Neither she nor Tins cared whether Mr. X arrived during the second or third settlement of the area, or whose daughter married whose son. It was bloody ages ago, and her grandfather's obsession with the Ryder-White line, when they had so much to achieve, was just silly, in her opinion.

She was busier than most of her family, and both

Mick Pritchard and Griff O'Hare were giving her indigestion for wildly different reasons.

Kinga scowled. Griff O'Hare was an enigma and she wasn't fond of puzzles. She liked her men straightforward and, well, let's be frank, a little pliable. Beta men were a fire suit, a measure of protection, because she knew she'd never fall in love with a man she could boss around.

She didn't like change or risk or danger, and Griff O'Hare, damn him, was all three wrapped up in one luscious package.

He was a man whose kisses set her soul on fire and who made her feel out of control.

After what happened with Jas, control was paramount. Kinga would never risk loving and losing someone again.

Like her best friend, Griff was a charismatic, pull-to-a-flame creature. She had to be on guard around him. Her attraction to Griff, to the wildness she sensed in him, was dangerous. If she lowered her guard, she could make a mistake that could have enormous consequences.

To her ball, to her reputation and, if she weren't very, very careful, her heart.

So, no more kissing, touching or wondering what he looked like under his clothes.

Kinga yawned and closed the lid to her laptop. It was way after midnight and she should climb the stairs and go to bed. She had a long day tomorrow. With O'Hare invading her dreams and providing her with some X-rated fantasies, sleep wasn't something she was getting a lot of lately.

Kinga placed her laptop on her coffee table, switched off the table lamp and stood up. She padded over to the door to check that all four locks were engaged—she knew they were locked but she wouldn't sleep unless she'd checked. About to turn to walk up the stairs, she heard a sharp rap on her front door. With her heart trying to escape through her throat, she stood statue-still, wondering who could be banging on her door at—she glanced at her watch—twelve thirty in the morning.

Another knock and Kinga heard Griff's soft voice calling her name. Kinga bent over, placed her hands on her thighs and breathed deeply, trying to push the panic away. God, maybe she should've stayed longer in trauma counseling.

Pulling in a deep breath, and telling her heart to calm the hell down, Kinga checked her peephole and sighed. Even distorted, Griff looked lovely. She flipped open her locks, pulled the door ajar and immediately inhaled the divine scent of garlic, melted cheese, herbs and fresh tomato.

Griff held a pizza box in his hand and a cake box in the other, both bearing the logo of the famous restaurants in New York.

He'd heard her request and had made the effort to fulfill it.

Holy crap, who was this man?

Kinga opened the door and took her time examining Griff. He wore faded blue jeans and a light blue open-neck shirt. His buttoned waistcoat was a deep brown and his jacket a rich cream. Classic, brown Oxford leather shoes covered his feet. His coat and scarf lay on the wooden bench pushed up against the outer wall of her apartment.

He looked amazing, as yummy as the pizza smelled.

Kinga lifted her eyes to his face and her stomach lurched at the now-familiar half smile she saw on his face.

"You brought me pizza and cheesecake," Kinga stated. She reached for the pizza box, suddenly conscious of how hungry she was. "Thank you. That's sweet… Gimme."

Griff flashed *that* smile, the one that revealed those amazing dimples and, after a bit of tugging, allowed her to take the flat box from his hands. Kinga turned and walked back into her apartment, flipping open the lid. In a well-practiced move, she held the box with one hand, lifted and folded a slice of pizza, and had the slice in her mouth before she reached the sofa.

Sinking to sit cross-legged on her coffee table— she didn't want the greasy pizza anywhere near her silk sofa cushions—she closed her eyes as the intense flavors hit her tongue.

If there was no New York–style pizza in heaven, she wasn't going.

Kinga heard Griff close her door, heard the locks turning and then saw him cross the room to sit on the sofa in front of her. He placed the box of cheesecake on the table and tried to tug the pizza box from her tight grip.

"You dined at Frodo's. You shouldn't be hungry."

Griff scoffed at that statement. "Geraint's portions are bite-size and, while stunning, were just enough to satisfy an overweight flea." He tugged at the box again. "Have a heart, Ryder-White, my stomach is eating itself."

Kinga released her grip on the box and Griff helped himself. Like her, he folded his pizza in half and took a huge bite, demolishing half the slice. Without talking, Kinga and Griff steadily made their way through the bulk of the pie, only talking to murmur their approval of their late-night treat.

There were two slices left in the box and Kinga picked up a napkin to wipe her greasy hands. She still wanted cheesecake, but was rapidly running out of room. Griff, big and bold, didn't have that problem. She leaned back on her hands and dropped her legs off the coffee table, her knees on the inside of Griff's. She felt sated and a little sleepy, and her eyes wandered over Griff, taking in his strong neck, the stubble on his cheeks, the intensity of his eyes. He had a tiny drop of tomato sauce on his lovely, pale blue shirt and Kinga used her index finger to scoop up the drop before it stained.

Except that the stain was dry.

She frowned and sat up straight, her eyes narrowing. "Mine wasn't the first pizza you ate tonight, was it, O'Hare?"

"I have no idea what you are talking about." Griff's innocent look didn't fool her for a second.

Kinga leaned forward and bent to the side to look in the direction of his ass.

"What are you doing?" Griff asked, puzzled.

"Checking to see if your pants are on fire," Kinga retorted. "Mmm, let me guess. While you were at Frodo's, you and Stan sent a minion to Lombardi's to order a couple of pies. One or two of which you ate on the plane on the way home. Or in the taxi on the way to the airport."

Griff grinned at her. "Busted."

"And then you ate half of mine!" Kinga pointed at the box, struggling to keep from smiling. "You jerk!"

Griff popped the last bite of his slice into his mouth and when he swallowed, he shrugged and smiled at her. "At least I brought you a whole pizza. I was tempted to eat some of it on the way over here."

"Lucky for you that you didn't," Kinga tartly responded.

"I could've not brought you any at all," Griff pointed out, that sexy smile still on his face.

It really was a sweet gesture. Had she thanked him properly? And thank him she should. Kinga leaned forward and touched her lips to his in a brief kiss. She placed her fingertips on his strong jaw before pulling back. "Thank you for the pizza," she softly told him. "It was a very nice of you to think of me."

"Even if I did eat most of it?" Griff asked, his voice raspier than normal.

"Even so," Kinga said before tapping her fingers against that sexy stubble. "But the cheesecake is mine."

Griff captured her fingers in his and gently, so very gently, kissed the tips. "Bet I could persuade you to share."

"Bet you couldn't."

This was, after all, Junior's cheesecake. She might not be able to finish a whole pizza pie, but she could scarf down an entire cheesecake with no problems at all. It was her superpower.

Griff's eyes darkened to intense green, the color of Maine woods after a hard rain. Kinga felt her throat tighten and her nipples harden. She was old enough, experienced enough to know that he was contemplating eating her sweet treat in a very non-conventional way.

It surprised her to realize she didn't have the slightest objection to combining food and pleasure…

Oh, there were a million reasons why sleeping with Griff was a mistake but, by all things holy, she couldn't remember one. The ache between her legs needed to be assuaged; her skin craved his touch. Her mouth needed his on hers—immediately—and her hand itched to strip those beautiful clothes from his stunning, masculine body.

Even her mind, normally so clear-thinking, was silent.

"Tell me what you are contemplating, Kinga," Griff asked her, scooting forward and wrapping his big hands around her thighs, just above her knees.

"I'm thinking that you would like to lick cheese-cake off me," Kinga whispered, surprised by her low, raspy phone-sex voice.

"You'd be right," Griff replied. "I've been having cheesecake-inappropriate thoughts since boarding the damn plane."

Feeling like she was operating outside of herself, Kinga flipped open the lid of the cheesecake box and, using her finger, scooped up a blob of filling and slowly sucked it off her finger. Griff's eyes followed her actions and Kinga dropped her gaze to see his erection tenting his pants.

Griff was a big man, everywhere.

"My turn," Griff said, echoing her actions. He smeared some filling down her neck and took his time licking her clean. Kinga heard someone's hard breathing, realized it was hers, and shuddered. She'd only sucked her finger and felt his lips on her neck, she shouldn't be this turned on...

Yet she was. And she had no intention of stopping...

Griff snapped off a corner of cheesecake, popped it into his mouth and then kissed her, deeply and with complete confidence. A million taste bombs exploded on her tongue. The tart tang of the cheesecake, a hit of sweetness, Griff himself.

As their tongues danced and dueled, Kinga went to work on his clothes, of which there were too many. She pushed his jacket off his shoulders, undid the buttons to his waistcoat and pushed both garments down his arms and flung them away. Under his thin cotton shirt she could feel his hot skin and, not wanting to waste time fiddling with buttons, she yanked it out of his jeans and pulled it over his head, exposing his gorgeously hard, tanned, muscular chest to her hands, eyes and mouth. Pulling back, she looked down to see a light smattering of hair, a darker trail snaking over his ladder-like stomach to disappear under the band of his jeans.

His hands were under her jersey, confident fingers exploring her breasts and stomach and, while she loved his touch, it was more important to trace the ball of his muscled shoulder with her tongue, to smear cheesecake across a flat nipple and lick it off, to hear him shudder and feel him squirm.

This hot, sexy, alpha man was completely under her spell and Kinga felt powerful, connected to the source of ancient, feminine wisdom and strength.

She was never the aggressor in sex, and rarely allowed her dates to go this far, but with Griff, she felt safe and…free. Free to explore, to be the initiator. He was strong enough, confident in his masculinity to allow her to take the lead…

Kinga stood up, pushed the coffee table away and put the cheesecake box on the floor, in easy reach. Kneeling between Griff's legs, she placed a palm on his chest and forced him to lean back. He watched her through hooded eyes as she tackled his soft leather belt and then the buttons on his jeans.

"You seem to be doing all the work, baby," he murmured, his hand cupping her cheek.

Kinga sent him a cheeky smile before placing her palm on his thick, steel-hard cock. "Do I look like I have a problem with that?"

"No," Griff replied, lifting his hips to push into her hand. "I love the way you touch me, Kinga."

His cotton underwear was a barrier, so Kinga pulled down his boxer briefs and there he was, six or seven inches of masculine glory. Dipping her head, she blew against his shaft, inhaling his fresh, clean smell. After nuzzling him and teasing him with eager fingers, she fumbled for the cheesecake box and scooped up a little filling, creating a cream-colored strip down the center of his shaft.

"I certainly hope you're going to lick that off," Griff muttered.

Kinga looked up at him, her lips quirking when she saw his forearm across his eyes, big biceps bulging. His breathing was shallow and the cords in his neck tightened.

Oh, yeah, she was so in control here. She liked it. Of course she did, control was her thing...

But she'd never exerted control in this particular way. Up until now, fellatio wasn't in her box of sexual tricks. Oral sex was so very intimate, more so than regular sex, and she'd never hit that level of comfort before...

Strange that she wanted to share this with Griff, that he was the man who made her feel so at ease...

Griff, gorgeous and hot, made her act differently. Later, when her brain returned to normal, she'd work out what that meant. And how to protect herself. But right now, all she wanted was to taste him. Using her tongue, Kinga licked off the filling, surprised at how hot he was, how hard. She'd heard the expression, velvet over steel, and while it was a cliché, it was a perfect description for his lovely erection.

Her hand enveloped him and she licked around the tip before taking him into her mouth...

"That's it, no more," Griff muttered, launching himself up. Using his strength, and he had lots of it, he lifted Kinga to her feet, pulled down her yoga pants and ordered her to take off her thin jersey.

Still trying to get her bearings, she hesitated and looked down, her eyes slamming into Griff's. All pretense of teasing and fun was gone—he was now a man on a mission. Hopefully that mission was to make her scream...

Then, as she stared at him, his eyes softened and his hands came to rest on her hips, his thumbs drawing patterns on her skin. "Do you want this, Kinga? Do you want me? Because if you want to stop, this is a good time."

Did she want to stop? *No*.

Should she? *Hell, yes*.

But she knew she wouldn't. She wanted to know what making love with Griff was like. If she walked away now, she'd regret it forever.

Griff must've seen something on her face—eagerness? consent?—because his mouth curled up into that sexy smile-smirk. "Good, because we haven't finished eating the cheesecake."

Kinga looked down at the mangled cheesecake and smiled. "No, we haven't, have we?"

Griff's expression turned serious again. "Does that mean I can make love to you?"

Kinga didn't hesitate. She just nodded before lowering her head to brush her mouth across his. "Yes. Let's do a threesome…you, me and the cheesecake."

His laughter created a deep warmth inside her and she couldn't help her long sigh as he undid the front clasp of her bra and gently pulled the cups aside. The heat of his mouth tugging on her nipple raised her temperature further and she clasped her hand to the back of his head, arching her back as he pleasured her.

He lifted his head to speak, his expression rueful. "I need you, Kinga, but I'm not carrying any condoms. Got any upstairs?"

That was easy to answer. "No."

Disappointment flashed in his eyes, across his face. She couldn't bear the thought of stopping now, not knowing what making love to him would be like. She needed to know him. "But, if you can promise me you're clean, I am on the pill."

He placed his hand on his chest and nodded. "I am, I promise."

She swallowed, suddenly a little shy. All she could do was nod.

Griff didn't hesitate, taking her mouth while dropping his jeans and underwear. He slid his hands between her legs, his thumb brushing her most sensitive area. Pulling back to look at her, he lifted her leg, held it across his hip and nudged her opening with his cock, sliding inside her.

She gasped, entranced by the look in his eyes and the wonder on his face. She'd never had a man look at her like that, ever…a combination of heat and wonder and pleasure and satisfaction. Like she was all his birthdays and Christmases rolled into one.

Being the object of such intense fascination sent tingles up her spine, and she felt that lift of the wave, the need to soar, then crash.

Kinga could feel Griff's tension, heard his groan and then he spun her around to sit her on the back of the couch, lifting her legs. It was instinctive to wind her legs around his waist, to arch her hips into his and with one deep thrust, he hit a spot that sent her skyward before exploding into a Catherine wheel of sparkles and sensation.

She heard his shout, felt his shudder but her world was still whirling and spinning. This was good sex, no, this was spectacular sex.

This was a mind-blowing, soul changing, impulsive coupling that could, if she wasn't very, very smart, shake the foundations of her world.

And, in doing so, could upend the stable, controlled life she worked so hard to create.

Griff O'Hare was a game changer but she couldn't let him change her. As she'd realized earlier, he was risk and danger.

Her arms wrapped around his neck, Kinga silently prayed to find a way to protect herself.

# Six

*Penelope*

Penelope looked down at her six-carat diamond engagement ring, surrounded by emeralds from ancient Ceylon, now Sri Lanka, passed down through the Ryder-White clan to the wife of the oldest son. She was the fifth—or was it the sixth?—Ryder-White wife to wear the magnificent and irreplaccable jewel.

Like so much else about her life, she both loved and hated it. Loved that the jewel was rare and stunningly expensive, hated it because it was another stupid Ryder-White tradition and neither of her daughters would one day wear the ring. Her father-in-law had made it clear that it was on loan to her.

Bloody Callum.

Through force of will, Penelope kept her spine steel-rod straight, her clasped hands resting on the cheap vinyl table in a diner on the west side of town. She'd refused coffee, asked for water, and pushed away the menu with one finger, the tip of which was perfectly painted in bright fuchsia.

This wasn't her usual milieu. She didn't know how to relate to blue-collar folk but this meeting required anonymity and discretion. Nobody would expect Penelope Ryder-White, society wife and fund-raising maven, to frequent this slightly grubby, riot-ously busy truck stop on the edge of town.

Penelope removed her designer sunglasses, carefully folded them and tapped the edge of the frame against the table. She'd been waiting for five minutes already and her contact was late. She abhorred tardiness and would wait for, precisely, another five and then she would leave. And then she'd find another private investigator, someone who could, at the very least, be punctual.

Finding an investigator wasn't hard; finding one who could give her quick results was trickier. Callum was becoming increasingly difficult. Things were changing and she needed information to anticipate and head off trouble.

A middle-aged, curvy woman holding a coffee cup dropped onto the bench seat opposite her and shoved her own, cheap sunglasses into bright red hair. With her deep green eyes, freckles, a wide mouth and lack of makeup, she looked like any other suburban housewife.

Penelope raised her thin eyebrows in displeasure. "Excuse me, that seat is taken."

Amusement flashed in her eyes. "Ms. Ryder-White, I'm KJ Holden."

She was KJ Holden, reputed to be one of the best investigators in the city? This woman was a whiz at tracking down missing people and family members?

She didn't think so.

"You?" Penelope demanded.

With an annoyed sigh, KJ lifted her bottom and pulled a thin wallet from the back of her pants. After flipping it open, KJ eased a card from a slot and pushed it across the table. The card told Penelope that she was a registered PI and bail bonds agent.

Right, so much for assumptions. "You must get that a lot," Penelope said. It was as close as she could come to an apology. People of her ilk and wealth weren't in the habit of dropping *sorrys* like snowballs.

"Normally people are politer," KJ said on a false smile.

She was feisty, too. Penelope rather liked that. Her daughters were feisty and fierce and she liked that they were strong and independent women. Like Callum, Pen looked down on pacifists and suck-ups. Her husband was, unfortunately, both.

"I'm not going to be able to help you if you don't tell me what the problem is, Ms. Ryder-White."

Penelope tucked her hair behind her ears and fiddled with the diamond stud in her ear. "I understand that you have a good reputation for finding the missing, but also for making connections between people and companies."

"I do," KJ replied. Her words weren't a boast but a statement of fact.

"Did you ever work on the Jas Garwood case?" Penelope asked, curious. Jas's hit-and-run death had turned Kinga into a tightly controlled, fearful adult.

KJ shook her head. "I specialize in looking for the missing. However, I know the detective working the cold case and there are no leads on the driver of the vehicle. They've chased down everything, I don't think there's anything to be found." KJ tipped her head to the side. "Your daughter was her best friend, right?"

Penelope nodded. "Since kindergarten. Jas all but grew up in our house and the Garwoods consider Kinga their second daughter."

"I'm very sorry," KJ said. She tapped her finger against her coffee cup and wrinkled her nose.

Pushing her coffee cup away, she leaned back in her seat and met Penelope's gaze. Her face and body might fool people into thinking she was a harried mom, but her eyes had seen trouble and were a hundred years old. Those eyes reassured Penelope that this woman could get the job done.

"What can I do for you, Ms. Ryder-White?"

Ah, could KJ give Penelope's father-in-law a personality transplant? But this woman was a PI, not a fairy godmother with a wand.

Penelope bit her bottom lip, unsure if she should proceed. Would she be opening up Pandora's box?

Would hiring a PI make everything better or worse? She didn't know...

But living on eggshells was driving her insane.

"Ms.—"

"Give me a minute," Penelope snapped. She just needed some time to *think*.

For what felt like forever, she'd been waiting to hear from the son she'd given up for adoption thirty five years ago. Once he turned eighteen, she'd expected a phone call asking for an explanation, asking who his father was. It was a long time to wait...

And a long time to worry about whether her youthful, scandalous affair would come to light.

She and her lover had been guests at a beach house in the Hamptons. She'd been intrigued by the much older man, flattered. She'd felt sophisticated, so very grown-up. He'd been stunningly good-looking, funny and, as a shy girl with overprotective parents, she'd been easily charmed out of her clothes. But on leaving the Hamptons, he'd ghosted her. She'd never felt so scared, so alone in her life. Like the Ryder-Whites, her family were East Coast blue bloods... rich, wealthy, stunningly *correct*. Girls from her social standing didn't get pregnant. Appearances had to be maintained.

*That* hadn't changed in three-plus decades. Appearances were still everything.

Gathering all her courage, she'd told her parents she was pregnant, clever enough to know that she could never name the father of her unborn child. As she expected, they assumed she'd had an affair with the pool boy or the gardener, someone much lower down the social ladder. She didn't bother to correct them.

After they stopped shouting, they flew into action.

Tickets to England were bought, an apartment in London rented. Numb, sick, sad and overwhelmed, she allowed them to contact the Knightsbridge adoption agency, met with the officials. Her parents wanted a completely closed adoption. She refused to sign any papers until she had their agreement that her son, should he wish to do so, could contact her when he was an adult. She lived in anticipation— and dread—of receiving a call, a letter, an email... something.

She'd heard nothing.

That baby would turn thirty-five soon, in less than a month.

Eighteen months after leaving London, she ran into her lover and during a furious argument, told him she'd given his son up for adoption. She'd never, before or since, seen anyone that angry. He'd demanded to know where the baby was, vowed to track him down. She tried to explain that the adoption was completed, that he had no chance of getting the baby back but he, being who he was, refused to accept that. The best she could do was give him the name of the adoption agency in London.

That was the last time she saw him and she had no idea what plans he put in place, what measures he'd taken after that to find his son. Not knowing almost drove her mad.

And why hadn't her son reached out? Wasn't he curious about the circumstances of his birth? Did he know and was just ignoring her? Had he chosen not to find out? And if so, why?

She couldn't live with uncertainty anymore, she had to find him, and when she did, she needed a private investigator who could do a deep dive into his life. Was he the type to exploit his connection to the famous family she was a part of? If yes, she needed to mitigate the fallout.

She never wondered whether he'd had a good life and a decent education, as the adoption agency they used only dealt with the extremely wealthy. And she tried not to think about whether he was happy and loved. She hoped he was, but since she couldn't do anything to change his circumstances, she always pushed those fears away. What good did it do to worry about something she couldn't change?

But she couldn't help wondering about him, who he was. Was he married or did he have kids? Was she a *grandmother*? What did he do for a job? Was he healthy? Did he look like his birth father or her?

Penelope rubbed her forehead and rolled her shoulders. Those questions, like a million more, were unproductive and useless. Unless he got in touch with her—and with every year that passed that possibility became more remote—she'd never know.

But she couldn't stop thinking about possible connections…and the consequences of her youthful actions. Penelope believed in having advance warning, a backup plan. And yes, if she could swing it so that she came out with her reputation intact—keeping her secrets—that would be a huge win.

"I need you to find a child I gave up for adoption a long time ago," Penelope told KJ, pushing the paper across the table.

She ignored the PI's raised eyebrows and the surprise flashing in her eyes. Yes, she'd had a baby when she was still a teenager, many had and many would. "It was a closed adoption, so I have no information on him."

KJ read the document and when she lifted her eyes to Penelope's again, she looked skeptical. "That might be difficult, especially since this adoption agency is based out of London. What's the deadline?"

"Yesterday."

"Of course it is," KJ said, releasing a heavy sigh.

Penelope was done with this conversation, with wading around in the muck of her past, and with this dreadful diner. "I've written down everything I know about him and the circumstances of his birth. Do not bother to contact me looking for more information. There isn't any." Penelope tapped the table with her index finger. "Find him, and I will pay you triple your rate with a big bonus."

KJ picked up the paper, read through the scant information again and raised her eyebrows. "Are you sure you want to kick over this rock, Mrs. Ryder-White?"

Penelope narrowed her eyes. "I wouldn't be meeting you here if I wasn't."

"I make a point of reminding my clients that the truth doesn't always set them free," KJ told her, flicking the paper with her thumbnail.

But secrets could also bury you alive, Penelope thought, before ending the meeting.

Kinga followed Studio Portland's manager down a wide hallway and thanked him when he opened the door to a vast studio space and gestured for her to enter. Stepping inside the huge room, she took in the action: scruffy band members milling about on the full stage, others setting up equipment, someone banging away on a set of drums.

Not seeing Griff, she turned in a full circle, observing the wooden area in front of the stage for dancers, the natural lighting flooding in from the bank of large rectangular windows to her left. She eventually found Griff sitting on a couch at the back of the room, a writing pad on his knee and a sexy pair of wire-framed glasses on his gorgeous face.

Kinga leaned her shoulder into the wall, taking a moment to study the man she'd slept with a week before. She hadn't seen him since he left her apartment very early the next morning, slipping out of her bed with a kiss on her forehead and zero explanations. They'd spent a crazy, wild, hot night together—God, it had been the best sex of her life—but she hadn't wanted any morning-after awkwardness. Neither had she wanted to discuss how they were supposed to act going forward.

He'd left Portland and this morning she'd received

a message informing her he was back. She tapped her fingers against her heart, feeling both excited to see him and confused about how to act. While he was away—she had no idea where he'd gone, and refused to ask—they'd exchanged many work-related text messages, and if she could carry on having a text-based relationship with him until the ball, she would. It was so much cleaner, easier.

*Safer.*

If they kept their distance, she could pretend he was just another artist—one of the many she'd dealt with over the years—and not someone who rocked her sexual world.

Kinga lifted her fingertips to her forehead, wishing she could get his beautiful body, and the way he made hers sing, out of her mind. She hadn't had a decent night's sleep since he'd spent the night in her bed. Despite washing her linens and her towels, she could still, strangely, smell his citrus cologne, taste cheesecake on her tongue and hear the deep rumble of his voice. In her dreams, he often made love to her. Frustratingly, her subconscious always took her to the brink before waking her up. She was horny, tired and deeply frustrated.

Not that she'd ever let him know that.

He was such a contradiction, Kinga thought, happy to watch him. He had a rock star vibe, completely confident and effortlessly stylish, but still managing to exude an alpha male, don't-screw-with-me attitude. He was charming and had a wicked sense of humor, but below the surface, she sensed dark and turbulent waters. Kinga suspected he had a complicated backstory, depths that had never been explored, feelings and thoughts that went unuttered.

There was Griff O'Hare, the wild musician, stupendously talented, and there was the real Griff, private and intense and so very…real. She could dismiss and ignore the artist, but the man behind the facade fascinated her.

Like the rest of the world, Kinga wanted to know why he acted out, what motivated his bad boy behavior, why he'd given up music and performing to hibernate on his ranch for a couple of years. She wanted to know about his family—never discussed by him—and she wanted to know whether he'd ever thought about changing careers. Was he where he wanted to be? Was he living the life he wanted?

Was she?

Good question. Kinga stared down at the toes of her spiky-heeled, thigh-high boots. Callum had carved out a space for her and Tinsley at Ryder International, but despite her MBA, her two degrees and years in the business, Kinga knew neither she nor Tinsley would ever be promoted into the CEO position. Neither, sadly, would her dad.

She adored her father, but James was too soft to make the hard decisions a multinational company needed. Someone who operated at that level needed to be focused, unemotional, fiercely intelligent and, to an extent, ruthless.

Her father was intelligent but emotional, and unlike Callum, James didn't have a ruthless bone in his body.

Years ago, after leaving college, Kinga had campaigned hard to get her grandfather to consider her as his successor but he'd either brushed her off or laughed at her ambitions. She was a woman and, as such, lacked the "balls" the job needed—his expression. Her ego had been hurt and her pride scorched, but when she pushed both away, she realized that she didn't really want the responsibility or the stress of leading Ryder International.

She didn't want to end up old and brittle, a workaholic, putting profits above people. Cold, disengaged, soulless.

She didn't, in other words, want to be like Callum.

Kinga felt her phone vibrate and looked at the screen, smiling when she saw her sister's number. "Hey."

"Why did you support Callum's decision to appoint Cody Craigmyle's company to co-create and manage the cocktail competition?"

Kinga winced at the venom in her sister's voice. "Because his quote was very competitive, he has experience in running international events, does fantastic work and has never, *ever* let us down."

Tinsley didn't respond, so Kinga spoke again. "He's also someone we've known most of our lives and we trust him."

"*You* trust him," Tinsley muttered.

Kinga shook her head. Even as teenagers, Tinsley and Cody had been combative, but since her divorce from Cody's younger brother, JT, their animosity had ratcheted way up. Before marrying, Tinsley and JT had been an item through high school and into college; the Ryder-Whites and the Craigmyles were close friends and trusted business associates. And best of all, Callum had approved of and promoted the marriage. Kinga had thought that JT and Tinsley had a good chance of making it over the long term.

They hadn't. Now Tinsley was single again, her ex was living in Hong Kong and had remarried and—pouring peroxide onto her torn-up heart because Tinsley had begged him to start a family—had a baby on the way.

Tinsley's marriage was over and she never spoke to JT anymore. Tinsley and Cody, however, would not stop arguing. Kinga wondered if Tinsley was taking out her hurt and anger over the divorce on Cody. But she wasn't brave enough to suggest that to Tinsley. Kinga just wished the two would stop bickering or, if that was impossible, to leave her out of it.

They exhausted her.

"The contracts have been signed and you are overseeing the mixology competition, so you're going to have to work with him," Kinga told her sister.

"I don't want to," Tinsley said, sounding like the sulky five-year-old she'd once been.

"Deal with it, babe," Kinga told her before disconnecting the call. Shoving her phone back in her leather tote bag, she looked up to see Griff looking at her from his seat on the couch, that sexy smirk on his face.

Kinga walked over to him, conscious of the heat in his eyes. She'd pulled on thick black tights and a gray turtleneck sweater dress that ended six inches above her boots and Griff seemed fascinated by the space between her hem and her boots.

"Hi," he said, standing up as she approached him. To her surprise, he placed his hand on her forearm and bent his head to drop a kiss on her temple. "How are you? You're looking tired."

There was genuine concern in his voice and interest in his eyes and because of both, Kinga answered him honestly. "I *am* tired."

"Working like a demon?" Griff said, gesturing for her to sit next to him on the leather sofa.

She couldn't tell him that most of her exhaustion was due to her vivid sex dreams, so Kinga just sat down and crossed her legs. She looked toward the stage, where the musicians were gathering, laughing and joking.

Kinga gestured to the stage. "I see you have a band."

Griff sat down next to her and rested his forearms on his thighs, turning his head to look at her. "Yeah, most of the musicians I like to work with were available, thank God. The backup singers are new to me but they have experience."

Kinga looked at the notepad he'd tossed on the table, saw the pages covered in his chicken scratch and what she thought might be lyrics.

Despite not wanting to invade his privacy, she

nodded to the writing pad before looking away. "Are you writing again?"

Griff's sigh was long and loud. "Mmm. I've been thinking about releasing an album of my compositions."

Kinga swiveled on the couch to face him. "That's fantastic!"

Griff grimaced. "It might be, if I knew if the songs were any good."

It was so strange to hear the usually confident man sound so uncertain. "I'm sure they are great, Griff. I mean, the last album you released went platinum."

"That was a while ago, Kinga," Griff responded, looking troubled. "And I had a cowriter." He placed his hand on the notepad. "This is all me…"

"I can't imagine how hard it must be to put your creations out in the world," she mused. "I suppose it must be like having a baby and putting his picture on social media and asking the world to comment on whether he's ugly or not."

Griff stared at her for a long time, his surprised expression eventually turning to amusement. "That's exactly what it feels like. I couldn't put it better myself." Griff took his glasses off and put them into the top pocket of his untucked button-down. Today's jeans were faded and thin, authentically aged, and he wore trendy, expensive sneakers on his feet. His hair was all over the place, probably because he'd spent the morning running his hands through it.

"How are your rehearsals going?" Kinga asked him.

"Good, mostly. I'm a bit rusty," Griff admitted. "It should go better now that I've finalized the set list."

"Will my grandfather approve?" Kinga asked him, knowing that Callum had very definite ideas on what music he wanted Griff to perform.

"I've gone for jazz and classic standards, very similar to a concert I did in London. But I've tossed in a couple of modern songs to keep the younger crowd happy."

Kinga twisted her lips. "I should warn you that my grandfather is planning to watch some of your rehearsals."

"That's not going to happen," Griff told her, his expression implacable. "Nobody watches me rehearse. Nobody but the band, dancers and crew are allowed into my practice studio."

"I'm here," Kinga pointed out.

"Not for long," Griff told her on a smile. He checked his watch, which was high-end and overly complicated. "I'm about to kick you out—the session starts in five minutes."

Kinga pouted and fluttered her eyelashes at him. "Just a few songs, please? I'll be as quiet as a church mouse."

Griff squinted at her. "Mmm. One song and then you leave."

Kinga bounced up and down, thoroughly excited. But if she only had five minutes, she needed to discuss business with him. Pulling her tablet from her bag, she powered it up before looking at Griff again. "Uh, a couple of quick questions. I've managed to book you onto a hugely popular morning talk show next week to discuss your comeback and the ball."

Griff looked like he'd rather be hanged, drawn and quartered. "The least favorite aspect of my work."

"Interviews are a necessary evil. So, what questions are off-limits? Same as for the press?" Kinga asked. She needed to produce a publicity pack for the talk shows and included in the briefing would be a list of dos and don'ts. Some interviewers pushed for more, but most respected the celebrity's privacy. None of them wanted to run the risk of losing trust and not being able to book interesting guests.

Griff rubbed his hand over his stubbled jaw. "Uh, same as last time. I definitely don't want to answer any questions about Sian."

His twin and his former costar. Kinga didn't know anything more about her than the man on the street. And she was curious, dammit.

"And I refuse to answer questions about my manager, his death or to comment on the rumors surrounding a supposed bust-up between us. They often try to sneak that question in."

Kinga heard devastation in his voice and noticed fury in his eyes. She tipped her head to the side, wondering, as so many did, why he refused to talk about the man he'd once called his second father, his mentor and his best friend. "Okay," she said.

"No questions about former lovers, my acting out, or that night in Phuket."

Kinga frowned. What was he talking about?

"What happened in Phuket? I didn't read anything about you visiting Phuket."

Griff grinned. "Ah, so you did read up on me?"

Kinga handed him a cool, get-over-yourself-smile. "I read the basics, O'Hare. I didn't do a deep dive into your life."

Griff dared to peek at her butt. "Now whose pants are on fire?"

"Jerk," Kinga muttered. She looked into his eyes, saw the desire blazing within them and placed her hand on her heart, silently telling it to slow the hell down. They'd made love, yes, but she was a modern woman. One hot, wild night did not a relationship make; it didn't even mean that he wanted a repeat.

It was just sex…

"I've been thinking about you," Griff told her, taking her hand and squeezing her fingers.

She couldn't deal with him looking and sounding so sincere. It gave her ideas and those she didn't need.

"You don't have to lie to me, O'Hare. I know exactly what that night was."

"And what was it, Kinga?" Griff asked her, his voice surprisingly gentle.

Kinga attempted a casual shrug, hoping to sound blasé. "A wild night, a step out of time, something that wouldn't be repeated."

"It was wild, it was unexpected," Griff admitted. "It's also a night that I can't stop thinking about. I can't stop thinking about *you*."

Yeah, she didn't believe that for one second. And

she was a little disappointed that Griff was treating her like a dumb groupie and not an intelligent, independent woman. Unlike a groupie, she wouldn't simper and melt when he used his sexy voice and bedroom eyes.

She wasn't romantic or impulsive. Starry-eyed and naive hadn't been her since she was eighteen and her world flipped upside down. She far preferred to see things how they were, not how she wanted them to be.

"You don't believe me," Griff stated, his voice low but intense.

Kinga heard a guitar riff, a drum roll and, glancing toward the stage, saw people taking their places. "You need to go. They're waiting for you."

"I am paying their salaries. They can wait until I am ready," Griff growled, and it was hard to miss his frustration. "Look, I didn't call you because I was out of town. I had…something to take care of."

Had he been called away by a woman, a longtime lover or a casual hookup? Did he leave to interview for a better job offer than what they'd offered for the ball? Was he about to ditch her? Or had he done something stupid while he was away, something that was still going to come to light?

*Stop, Kinga, you're overreacting and overthinking. Just…*

*Stop.*

She held up her hands, palms forward. "Griff, it's fine. I didn't expect you to call. I understand that this is, apart from one night, a completely professional relationship."

"Except that I want another night and possibly another night after that," Griff stated, his tone firm.

Kinga stared at him, unsure that she'd heard his words correctly. "Sorry?"

Griff bent down to speak directly in her ear and his breath warmed her neck. "I'd very much like to share your bed again, Kinga. Any chance of that happening?"

She pulled back to stare at him. She'd genuinely believed that he'd moved on to his next conquest, that she was just another woman on a long list. Why her?

She was tempted to throw caution to the wind and nod furiously, but her pride, and a healthy dose of wariness, wouldn't let her. She was about to ask him whether she could give his question some thought, when her phone rang. Deeply grateful for the interruption, she frowned at the unfamiliar number on the screen and answered.

"This is Edward, Senator Garwood's assistant. Hold for the senator please."

Kinga was very surprised to receive a call from Jas's father. He was in Washington and, as far as she knew, busy with a Supreme Court confirmation. Why was he calling her? She'd barely finished the thought when the answer popped into her head.

Mick Pritchard…

"Kinga, it's Seth."

Kinga heard his deep voice in her ear and smiled, as she always did. Jas's father loved his daughter and, because Kinga had been a fixture in his home for most of her life, loved her, too. "Uncle Seth. It's good to hear from you. Is everything okay?"

"That prick is back."

Seth rarely swore and his description of Mick told Kinga how upset he was at Mick's return.

"I know. He's called a few times and ambushed me in a parking lot. He wants you to support his bid for mayor."

"I'd rather shove a hot stick covered with fire ants up my ass," Seth told her, his voice vibrating with anger.

That would be a no, then. Just as she'd expected.

"The thing is, he managed to con his way onto the grounds of my house and Viola let him in. He told her that he wanted to talk to her about Jas, to reminisce. She's not making much sense, but it's obvious that he's upset her and she's having a meltdown."

Kinga knew what he was asking, without him having to say the words. Viola, sensitive and emotional, had a hard time regulating her emotions, even before Jas died. Now, few people could talk her down when she was in an agitated state. Seth was one of them, Kinga another.

"I'll go and see her, try and get her to calm down, maybe take a nap?"

Kinga heard Seth's relieved sigh. "Thank you, Kinga."

"I'll go now. Do you want me to call you and let you know she's okay?" Kinga asked, standing up and reaching for her bag.

"Please. You can get me on this number." Kinga heard the frustration in his voice and could easily imagine him pacing the floor of his office. Seth adored his wife and missed her terribly when the Senate was in session. "I swear, if I get my hands on that self-serving prick, I will rip his arms off."

"You and me both," Kinga told him. "I'll speak to you soon."

Kinga disconnected the call and abruptly dropped back down to the couch, feeling like someone had punched her in the gut. Looking down at her hands, she noticed that she was trembling. She had to pull herself together and make the trip across town to Cousins Island. Immediately. Viola needed her and she wouldn't repeat her mistakes and let her—or Seth—down.

But, God, the fear of failure was always there. And so was the urge to panic, dancing under her skin.

Kinga hauled in some much-needed air and saw a bottle of water in front of her face. Taking it, she cracked the lid, only to realize that it was already open. She took a big sip, then a deep breath, another sip, and felt a fraction calmer. She could do this...

Standing up, she picked up her bag and pulled it over her shoulder. Handing Griff the water bottle, she told him she had to go and, her arms wrapped around her waist, walked to the door.

*All this was her fault.*

The tendrils of panic grew stronger and she did not want to be behind the wheel of a car if an attack struck. If she became immobilized on the road, she could kill herself or someone else. And when she saw Viola, she needed to be clear-eyed and in control. She needed to do her deep breathing and calming exercises, but that meant having to hire a ride.

Kinga scrolled through her phone, eventually finding the contact number for the taxi company she routinely used. They were more reliable than a ride share service. She dialed, ordered a taxi, and when the dispatcher asked for a pickup address, she went blank.

She had no idea where she was…

Kinga felt her phone slide out of her fingers and lifted her eyes to look at Griff, his green eyes reflecting his confusion and concern. "Cancel the taxi, I'll drive you."

She looked around the room, seeing the musicians waiting for Griff, and shook her head. "You can't, all these people are here, you have a practice scheduled!"

"As I said, I'm the boss and pay their salaries." He looked across to the stage, sliced his hand across his neck and immediately, the band members realized that their session was canceled.

"Where do you need to go, baby?" Griff gently asked her, sliding her phone into the open pocket on the outside of her bag.

Kinga thought about lying but didn't have the energy. "I need to go to Senator Garwood's house on Cousins Island. It's about twenty minutes away. Will you take me?"

# Seven

A couple hours later, Griff followed Kinga into her apartment, gently closing the door behind him. He watched Kinga shrug out of her coat, hanging it up on the coatrack before turning to face her front door. He thought she was about to ask him to leave, but she turned the four locks on her front door instead.

She still looked pale, Griff thought, though not as white as she'd been when she joined him in his car after spending forty-five minutes within Senator Garwood's mansion. Griff rocked on his heels, desperate to pepper her with questions but not wanting to upset her further.

He wasn't particularly surprised that Portland's princess was on friendly terms with the state's first family, but he couldn't understand why the visit would upset her so much.

Deciding to give her some space, Griff looked at the raindrops hitting the windowpane and sighed. So far, Portland had two weather settings, snow and rain, both accompanied by wind. Kinga's apartment had great central heating but there was nothing like a fire to raise spirits. Wood sat in a neat pile next to the period-correct fireplace, so he walked over to the hearth and grabbed a handful of kindling.

Knowing that Kinga needed something to do, he asked her to make him a cup of coffee and set about adding logs to the hearth. By the time she returned with an espresso from her high-end machine, he had a healthy fire burning in the grate.

Kinga held out her hands to the warmth. "Thank you. I can't remember when last I used the fireplace."

Griff placed his cup on the table behind him and gently pulled her into his arms. Holding her, he wondered if he had any right to ask her the questions burning a hole in his brain. After all, he hadn't told her, or anyone, why he'd abruptly left Portland the morning after spending an enthralling, smoking-hot night in her bed.

No one besides his immediate family knew that in Key Largo, Sian had decided to take an early-morning swim, which wouldn't have been a problem if she'd stopped, turned around and headed back to shore. She hadn't. If Pete hadn't seen her when he stepped out onto his balcony shortly after waking up, Sian would've been halfway to Australia by the time they discovered her.

And dead.

Pete, a strong swimmer, had guided her back to shore and they'd immediately contacted her psychiatrist and Griff. A few hours after hearing from Pete, and after a detour to pick up Sian's therapist, he was on his way to Key Largo.

After spending hours with Sian, Dr. Warfield concluded that Sian experienced a rare schizophrenia-induced delusion. Her meds were adjusted, and by the time Griff left the island a week later, Sian was happier and chattier. Her disease was a roller coaster, Griff thought for the umpteenth time.

With Jan and Pete insisting that Sian, Sam and Eloise remain on the island with them, he'd hired a psychiatric nurse to monitor Sian for the duration of her visit. After the therapist left, Griff had hung around for a few more days, playing with and watching over Sam and catching up with his sisters and brother-in-law, telling them about his return to performing.

Sam was in his element, completely spoiled by Jan's girls, and it was obvious that he wasn't suffering from any lack of attention in Jan's household. They doted on him and Griff suspected that when Sam returned home, he might have a bit of a monster on his hands.

Thank God the press had no idea that Sian and Sam were in the Keys.

Walking backward, with a fragrant and soft woman still in his arms, Griff lowered himself to the nearest sofa and pulled Kinga down to sit on his lap. She curled up against his chest, her face in his neck. He rubbed her back and waited for her to speak.

He wouldn't force her to talk. He hated being interrogated and suspected she did, too.

Griff yawned and played with the edges of her supple boots. Thinking she'd be far more comfortable without her footwear, he eased the stretchy boots off her legs. Pulling her closer to his chest, he placed his hand on her thigh, his thumb drawing patterns on the inside of her knee. "Better?"

"Mmm, thanks."

He was curious, sure, but he could just sit here with this woman in his lap, her perfume wafting up to his nose, with the fire crackling and the rain turning to sleet as it smacked the windows. Sliding down a little, Griff rested his head on the back of the sofa and idly hummed the melody to a song he'd been working on earlier.

"That's nice," Kinga murmured.

"I thought you said you aren't musical," Griff gently teased her.

"I'm not, but that doesn't mean I can't enjoy a nice tune."

Griff's lips twitched at the hint of haughtiness in her voice and hoped it meant she was feeling a little better, a tad stronger. He decided to risk a probing question. "Can you tell me why you rushed over to Senator Garwood's house in the middle of a Tuesday afternoon?" he asked.

Kinga shot up and winced. "Oh, God, I spoiled

your practice session and you wasted all that time. I'm so sorry… The band and rental of the studio must be prohibitively expensive and I took you away."

Griff pulled her back down, tightened his arms around her and dropped a reassuring kiss in her hair. He was one of the highest-paid artists in the industry, and one afternoon's wages and studio rentals were less than petty cash to him. Not that he'd tell Kinga that—he'd sound like a boastful jerk.

"You were upset and you needed someone to drive you. I'm sorry I couldn't deliver you to the door, but reporters were hanging around and that would've started a media story neither of us needed," he added.

When he approached the senator's impressive gates, he'd seen a blond-haired man talking to the sizable number of reporters on the sidewalk. Judging by Kinga's feral growl, he assumed she recognized him but she gave no explanation of who he was or why he was there. Grateful the journalists weren't paying the traffic any attention, and for the tinted windows of his car, he drove past, turned down a side road and suggested that Kinga walk the short distance to the house. Telling her that he'd pick her up at the house when the coast was clear, he had spent the next forty-five minutes in his car, catching up on returning calls and emails and trying to ignore his growing curiosity.

Thankfully, the press had departed by the time Kinga was finished and he could pick her up without any cameras flashing or people yelling his name.

"Thank you for thinking of that—I certainly

didn't. And thank you for driving me," Kinga said. She lifted herself off his chest and rested her back against the arm of the sofa. She tucked her clasped hands between her thighs and when her eyes met his, he winced at the pain he saw within those honey-colored depths. "So…"

Griff didn't push her when she hesitated; he just waited for her to continue. When she did, her voice trembled. "The girl in that photo, the one on the mantel…that's Jas, Senator Garwood's daughter. She was my best friend, and we bonded on our first day in kindergarten. Tinsley and I are close now, but we weren't when we were kids. When she was sixteen, Tinsley and JT fell in love and they became inseparable and she didn't have much time for me. But Jas was always there—she was my soul sister and the other half of me. I don't know if you can understand that…"

He'd grown up in the limelight, on stages and TV and movie sets, and Sian had been his constant companion. And to an extent, his only friend, so, yeah, he understood. "I have a twin, remember?"

"Right," Kinga pushed her hand through her hair. "Ten years ago, Jas had just broken up with her boyfriend, Mick Pritchard, for the fourth or fifth time that year. We went to a New Years' party not far from Jas's house and my parents' estate… Well, it's my grandfather's estate…"

She was rambling and Griff let her go at her own pace.

"Callum wants you to come to dinner on Friday

night, by the way," Kinga said, and he blinked at her unexpected change of subject.

He lifted his eyebrows. "Will you be there?" he asked. If he could hold Kinga's hand under the table, he might consider it. Otherwise, there was no way he'd endure a meal with her cold, austere grandfather.

Kinga looked affronted. "Of course I will. There's no way I'd let you face my family alone."

He smiled at her protective attitude and didn't bother telling her that he'd been dealing with difficult, egocentric and self-important people most of his life. He'd decide about whether to accept her grandfather's invitation later; right now he wanted to hear the rest of Kinga's story.

"You were telling me about your friend…" he prompted.

Kinga turned her head to look out the window and his heart clenched at her desolate expression. "I told her we'd see in the new year together and I promised her a lift home, but a guy I was into arrived at the party. He wanted me to leave with him and Jas encouraged me to go, as a lot of our friends were there and she was having fun. I told her to phone me if she needed a ride, but she told me that it was all good…"

Ah, the phrase she so hated. Griff swallowed, dread creeping over him. He thought he knew where this was going.

"She never called and I presumed she got a ride home with one of our many friends at the party. Someone remembered seeing her at the house around four a.m. We now know she left on her own and that she was a little drunk. It was a misty night, but it was a road she was familiar with. Jas loved to walk at night and her house was only a half mile down the road. My house was a half mile in the opposite direction. She was so close to home, Griff."

"But she never made it."

"Initially we thought she'd been taken by a predator and we immediately put up missing person flyers and Seth—Senator Garwood—hired a private investigator. A few days later, they found her body in a deep ditch, covered with snow. She was a victim of a hit-and-run collision."

Griff's hand tightened on her knee. The poor kid. Kinga started to speak but then snapped her mouth closed, misery in her eyes and all over her face.

She didn't need to say the words; he understood what she couldn't say. She blamed herself. Kinga, protective and loving, felt responsible for her friend's death. It wasn't logical but, in her mind, she'd left her friend at a party, after promising to take her home, and it was her fault Jas was gone.

Kinga wasn't responsible but Griff knew that was a conclusion she'd have to come to in her own time. It might take another decade or it might not happen at all.

After a few minutes' silence, he spoke again. "And the rushed visit to the senator's house today?"

Kinga rubbed her hands up and down her face. "That would take a bit more explanation."

Griff waited while she decided whether or not to give him the whole story, knowing that, to an extent, it was a referendum on whether she trusted him or not. He wanted her to trust him, he realized. He wanted her to hand him her thoughts and fears, her hopes and dreams. He wanted to be the place, and the person, she felt safest with.

Yeah, this connection to Kinga was turning a lot more complicated than he'd expected…

*Not clever, O'Hare.* He was halfway down that slippery slope and his brakes weren't working.

Kinga played with the hem of her dress, her thoughts in the past. "Earlier, I mentioned that Jas had a boyfriend. I grew up with Mick—I've known him all my life and so did Jas. Mick and I were friends, and at times, we were really close. Along with the Craigmyle boys, I considered him to be the brother I never had."

Kinga folded the hem of her dress up an inch, and then another inch, revealing more of her slim thigh covered in a thin black stocking. Were they fancy stockings, the ones held up by those strappy, lacy garter things?

Griff cursed himself, reminding himself that he was listening to Kinga tell him about one of the worst periods of her life and that he should be concentrating on her story, not her lingerie.

*Get a goddamn grip, O'Hare.*

"Jas and Mick hooked up when they were seventeen and they were on and off, as I said. They were off at the time she died. That's why he wasn't at the party." Kinga hauled in a deep breath. "For those first few days when we thought she was missing, Mick was beside himself, crying, on his knees praying... He was desperate to find her. As you can imagine, the networks picked up on the story pretty quickly. Seth's popular, Viola's beautiful and Jas was brilliant. It was...well, very newsworthy."

He'd seen coverage of some of the more high-profile murder and missing investigations and understood that certain stories got more coverage than others. A famous and much-liked politician's beautiful and brilliant daughter going missing? That would bring out national and international reporters...

"You were telling me about the boyfriend..." Griff prompted Kinga.

"Mick took every opportunity to talk to the press. Looking back, I now realize he was milking the situation. On day two of her being gone—she was found on day three—he started blaming me, telling anybody who'd listen it was my fault."

Griff winced. What a bastard.

But he still didn't understand what any of this had to do with her visit to Garwood's house this afternoon. He told himself to be patient and listen.

Kinga tensed and Griff knew he was about to hear something he wasn't going to like. "After her funeral, I was at home, alone... I can't remember where my parents were. Mick arrived and he started yelling at me, telling me that I destroyed all his plans, that he'd intended to marry Jas, that she was his ticket.

"I didn't know what he was talking about and I started yelling back, I was so sick of his crap. I told him that Jas had said they were done, permanently,

and that she was glad to have him out of her life."
Kinga hesitated, then softly told him that she'd been
punched.

It took Griff a few moments for the red mist in
front of his eyes to clear. "I'm sorry," he carefully
asked, "did you say he hit you?"

"Mmm-hmm. He's a big guy and I fell to the floor.
It hurt like hell."

Griff released a low growl. "Please, please tell
me where I can find the prick so that I can rip his
limbs off."

Kinga placed her hand on his and squeezed. "He
was the blond-haired guy outside the Garwood house
today, talking to the press." Kinga pulled her bottom lip between her thumb and forefinger, deep in
thought. A minute later she dropped her hand to
speak again. "It's all starting to make sense, actually."

He was glad she thought so, because he didn't
have a damn clue. All he knew for sure was that if he
was alone with Pritchard, one of them would die and
it wouldn't be Griff. Kinga was tall but slim, and the
guy he'd seen earlier was six-four and bulky. God,
even a pulled punch from him would've stung like a
bitch. He could've broken her cheekbone, made her
crack her head when she hit the floor...

"He's the owner of a private security company
with offices here and in Boston. On his website is a
video promoting his services and telling the world
why he got into private security, to help people because his, and I'm paraphrasing, love of his life was

killed in a hit-and-run accident. In the video, he also names and blames me. Every year he emails or texts me on her anniversary to reinforce that message."

The sniveling cockroach.

"I've been able to ignore him mostly, but now he's back and he's launching a bid for mayor, and he wants Seth's endorsement. He ambushed me in a parking lot recently, telling me that I owe him, and demanding that I set up a meeting with the senator."

He what? What the f—

"Now I think that back then, he was planning on using Jas to ride Seth's coattails," Kinga mused. "Seth can't stand him because he's refused to take that video down. We believe he's capitalizing on Jas's death. Mick went to see Viola today, Jas's mother. She's never fully recovered from Jas's death and mostly stays at home. She told me he bullied his way into the house, and immediately demanded that she talk to Seth, that Seth owes it to Mick to endorse him for mayor. She was distraught and scared and it took me a while to calm her down."

"Is the guy clueless?"

"He's something," Kinga admitted. "He tipped off the press and that's why they were there. I bet you that he hinted at an announcement about him entering politics to tease them. He would've told them he was visiting Viola as Jas's boyfriend, showing his respect on the tenth anniversary of her death. The press will pick up on the story—they love anything to do with Seth and Jas."

Griff lifted his hand to hold her chin, making

sure she was looking at him when he spoke again. He wanted no misunderstandings about this. "If he comes anywhere near you, I want to know about it, Kinga."

Kinga shrugged. "I appreciate the sentiment but the last thing you can afford, from a PR point of view, is to get into a showdown with Mick Pritchard, Griff." Kinga shrugged. "I can handle him."

But she shouldn't have to, and Griff wanted to make it very clear to Pritchard that any fight he picked with Kinga meant taking on him, too.

"I. Want. To. Know." Griff enunciated each word.

"Fine," Kinga huffed, but in that one word, he heard the exhaustion and emotion in her voice. She came across as tough and together on the surface, but his amber-eyed pixie was a lot more vulnerable than she allowed the world to believe. Feeling tenderness rise up inside of him—well, he thought it was tenderness—he wrapped his arms around her, pulled her in close and kissed the top of her head.

While he was in Portland, for as long as this lasted, she was his to protect.

Griff lifted his hand to stroke her cheek with the tips of his fingers. "I'm sorry this happened to you, Kinga, so sorry that you lost your friend."

Kinga blinked away her tears. "I still miss her, Griff. As much today as I did ten years ago."

Griff nodded, understanding grief didn't die over time. It changed, sure, but it never went away. He still missed his parents.

"I know what loss is like, how it can rearrange

the world. Death, and the emotions it brings, is never simple and comes in so many different shapes and forms."

Kinga rested her forehead against his. "I'm so grateful you are here. Thank you for staying."

"Always a pleasure," Griff murmured back. And it was. Honestly, there was no place he'd rather be than holding Kinga.

Pulling back, she looked into his eyes and he watched, fascinated, as sorrow turned to desire. His eyes darted to her mouth and back to her eyes and liquid want invaded his veins, warming him from the inside out.

Kinga straddled his thighs, lowering her head to position her mouth above his, but Griff's hand on her shoulder stopped her from lowering her head. "Problem?" she asked, frowning.

Time to be the good guy. Frankly, it sucked. "I want you, Kinga, but you're vulnerable and still upset. Maybe it's not a good time."

Kinga rested her palm on his cheek, her thumb swiping over the stubble on his cheek. "It's a great time. I need you, Griff, I need to feel alive and connected and..."

*Loved.*

Kinga looked into his mesmerizing eyes, shocked that she'd nearly allowed the L word to escape. Love wasn't something she'd ever imagined for herself, not in any shape or form. Love was a story society had been fed for far too long and it didn't exist, not really. Friendship did, as did companionship. Attraction, obviously, and flat-out lust. Couples hooked up for a variety of reasons—in her parents' case it was an amalgamation of wealth and power—but love? No, that was a myth.

"Are you sure, Kinga?" Griff asked, searching her face.

"Very," Kinga told him, sitting up and grabbing the edges of her dress to pull it over her head, exposing her torso to Griff's appreciative gaze. He lifted his big hand to her breast, his tan hand a lovely contrast to her pale skin and pale pink bra. Griff sat up and put his mouth to her nipple, tugging her into his mouth, his hand going down the back of her panties to explore her butt cheek. The thought that she shouldn't be feeling like this, not with Jas dead, popped into her brain. But she also knew that Jas would be the first person to tell her carpe diem, to seize the day and all that.

Besides, Jas would not be the type of girl who'd kick a sexy, sweet man out of her bed.

Griff pulled away, his expression a little fierce. "I'm going to make you feel so good, Kinga."

*Yes, please.* She could live with that.

Griff asked her to lie back down and when she did, he hovered over her, taking his time, looking at her. Unable to wait, Kinga cupped the back of his neck and pulled his head down, needing his kiss, his tongue in her mouth.

While he fed her kisses, Griff unhooked her bra and dropped it to the floor. He moved his hands down her body to stop at her ankles, before sliding them back up her body. After removing her tights and caressing her calves, knees and thighs, his hand went back to her butt, his skilled fingers sliding under her bottom, probing to stroke lightly between her legs. Kinga allowed her thighs to fall open, and she wondered if Griff would notice her damp panties.

Still kissing her, alternating between take-her-to-heaven kisses and gentle nibbles, Griff's hand skated back up and then down her chest and over her stomach to rest his palm on her mons. Kinga pulled in a harsh breath as he moved his mouth from hers to her bare breast, and his fingers slid underneath the band of her panties to access her warm, wet and secretive places.

"Let's get rid of these, okay?"

Not able to speak, she heard his gentle command to lift her hips and felt the fabric slide down, and then it was gone. Griff's fingers drifted through her small patch of hair and his fingers—urgent now—slid over and into her folds, unerringly finding her clit, causing her to release a turned-on moan. She pushed into his hands, needing more and needing it now.

"That's it, baby."

One finger probed and entered her, his thumb caressing that center of pleasure until she whimpered into his neck, begging for release. Kinga felt that wave of pleasure lifting her, fully in the grasp of lust's primal power. Griff bent down to kiss her breast again, to suck her nipple to the roof of his mouth and Kinga knew that she was close to coming, that the wave was about to crash. Sensing her approaching climax, Griff pulled back and slowed down, murmuring compliments against her mouth and skin.

He could've been speaking Swahili or Spanish, she had no idea. All she cared about was his trailing mouth on her body, his tongue dipping into her belly button, his big body hovering over hers, his mouth on her mound, his hands holding her legs apart.

That wave swelled again, shooting her up, and she hovered on its crest as he sucked her bud into her mouth. She waited, sobbing and begging his name, and when his fingers slid into her channel, she screamed, dropped and flew.

She tumbled, caught up in a maelstrom of warm, wet pleasure.

When she found solid ground, came back to herself, Kinga pulled him up and cradled his head into her neck, half sobbing from the pleasure of the experience.

"Best orgasm ever," Kinga whispered in his ear and felt his lips curve against her skin.

"That was just the warm-up act," Griff told her, lifting his head to grin at her.

"I'm so glad I bought a ticket to this gig," Kinga teased him. "But wonderful warm-up acts put pressure on the main performer. You're gonna have to up your game, O'Hare."

"Not a problem," Griff assured her.

And it wasn't. Griff O'Hare, yet again, gave her an incredible one-man show.

# Eight

On Saturday morning, Kinga sat across from Griff in the Ryder International Gulfstream as they made their way to Manhattan. In one of their many conversations lately, Griff had mentioned he'd like to see the venue for the ball and to meet with the sound people she'd hired. After making space in her packed schedule, Kinga commandeered the Ryder International jet to fly them to New York City.

She'd booked them into a suite within the luxurious, iconic Forrester-Grantham Hotel. Having attended Columbia University, she wanted to show him her favorite spots in the city. Hopefully, his presence would go undetected by the press.

Either way, it would be nice to get away from

Portland, the press, the Mick situation and her up-tight family for a day or two.

Kinga stretched, thinking that dinner at Callum's house last night—postponed from the previous week—had been a shit show. Her parents had been visibly tense and had barely spoken to each other the whole evening. Or to anyone else.

Callum had banged on and on about the delays in the DNA test, and Cody Craigmyle, a favorite of both Callum and her parents, had attended, exchanging barbs and insults with Tinsley like street vendors trading produce.

The only time Kinga relaxed during the whole evening was when Griff sat himself down at Callum's Steinway and played some jazz tunes from the fifties and sixties. Callum and James smoked cigars, Penelope made her way through another glass of chardonnay and Tinsley and Cody glared at each other from opposite sides of the room.

Her family was frequently tense and uptight but not normally that bad.

Kinga watched Griff scribbling in a notepad, glasses on his nose and humming a tune, oblivious, she was sure, to her presence. She crossed her legs, remembering how he'd held her hand under the table last night, telling her to relax when she tried to whisper an apology for her family's bad behavior. And curled up into the corner of Callum's sofa, listening to him play, had made her feel like she'd spent the day at a spa or on a sun-drenched holiday. Loose, relaxed, pretty damn happy. Griff O'Hare, the bad boy of rock and roll, could calm her down, boost her spirits…

She also found herself telling him things she'd never shared with anyone before. Nobody else knew that Mick had hurt her, that he sent her ugly texts and voice messages every year, that he still blamed her for Jas's death. She hadn't come close to sharing that with anyone, not even Tinsley. All her sister knew was that she'd had a scary encounter with a guy, resulting in her feeling skittish around men she didn't know.

So, why did she tell Griff?

Kinga rolled her head to the side to look out the window, clouds below them, wishing she was touching him, needing the connection. He had a million secrets, none of which she was privy to, and Kinga knew she felt more for him than he did for her.

That was a fine way to get her heart shattered.

What was it about him that so intrigued her? He wasn't the first good-looking guy she'd encountered. Was it his bad boy streak that attracted her? Maybe. But Kinga suspected he wasn't as spoiled or selfserving as the media made him out to be.

He could be hard-ass and humorous, intellectual and impossible. He was smart and savvy and very, very talented. But it was his ability to be both alpha and tender, stubborn and sweet that had her all tied up. He got her, in ways that nobody ever had since, well, Jas. Feeling that sort of connection terrified her. If she were smart, she'd bail now, while she still could, while her heart was still reasonably intact. Her brain thought that was a pretty good plan; her body wanted more of him.

Her heart, well, who the hell knew what that stupid organ wanted?

Kinga heard Griff shift in his seat and turned her head to look at him. She caught his eyes and slowly responded to his soft smile. He stood, crossed the space between them and dropped into the seat next to her. His mouth drifted across hers in a can't-wait-for-more kiss. Pulling away before they both got carried away, Griff leaned back in his seat and placed his hand on her knee.

His thumb stroked her through the material of her skinny jeans and his eyes were tender. "You doing okay?" Griff asked her, half turning to face her.

"I should be asking you that," Kinga pulled a face, "after our less-than-fun dinner last night."

"Is your family normally that…uptight?"

Kinga wanted to lie but couldn't. "They aren't known for being warm and fuzzy, but normally they are better behaved." She placed her hand on top of his, pushing her fingers between his. "Since Christmas, my parents have been acting weird. Something is going on with them."

"Like?"

She could tell him her suspicions. After all, he was privy to her biggest secrets. "I wonder if they are finally talking divorce."

Griff looked surprised. "And that doesn't upset you?"

Kinga pulled her hand away and lifted her leg to

drape it over his lower thigh. His hand curled around her knee and she leaned back against the padded armrest. "Actually, sometimes I wish they would go their separate ways. Theirs has never been a love match. They don't fight but they're not happy, either. But Callum wouldn't approve, so I doubt a divorce would ever happen. My dad is big on getting his father's approval."

"Because he's next in line to inherit?"

She liked Griff's blunt questions, the way he said what he thought without pussyfooting around the issue. "I'm sure that's part of it. But I don't think he'll ever be Callum's successor. I love my dad, Griff, but he's not tough enough to be the CEO of an international company worth a few billion. My mom, on the other hand, is tough, but she doesn't have the skills needed for the job."

"And you do."

Kinga nodded. "I do. But I don't want the job. I love what I'm doing now. The CEO position is twenty-four seven and I don't think I have the temperament for it, either."

Griff smiled. "Fair enough." He picked up his bottle of water, unscrewed the cap and took a long sip. "Why didn't your dad leave the business, pursue another career?"

*Pfft.* In Callum's world, that wasn't possible. James was his son and his son belonged in Ryder International, even if it meant chipping away at his soul every day. With Callum, doing things any other way than his way was never an option.

Kinga took his water bottle from his hand and sipped. Replacing the cap, she considered her words. "My grandfather is as tough as old leather and it's his way or the highway. I'll give you a classic example of how controlling he is…

"He had a brother, Ben, who was fifteen years younger than him. From what I can gather, rumors always abounded about Ben's sexuality and Callum couldn't accept that his brother was either bisexual or gay. Ben was, in Callum's eyes, embarrassing the family name.

"Callum and Ben ran Ryder's together at that time, but Callum wouldn't stop nagging Ben to find a wife and have a son. Ben finally confirmed all the rumors and told Callum that he'd fallen in love with the man he wanted to be with. Callum couldn't accept it, and he tried to force Benjamin out of the business."

"Harsh."

Kinga agreed.

"There was a huge family ruckus. It affected my father's relationship with Callum because my dad publicly supported his uncle. Ben died in a car crash before my parents married, I don't think my mom met him. Anyway, the authorities said he was speeding, that he had to have been distracted to end up dying in a one car accident. I think that my dad quietly blamed Callum for Ben's state of mind. He and Ben were close and my dad refused to obey Callum's order to cut him out of his life, and Callum has never forgiven him for taking Ben's side. Callum didn't even go to Ben's funeral when he passed away."

"That's quite a story," Griff said.

"Yeah, my grandfather is ruthless, controlling and old, *old* school. In fact, and don't take this the wrong way, I was surprised he had you around for dinner. My grandfather doesn't generally have much time for supposed degenerates and reprobates."

A strange look crossed Griff's face. "Maybe he hasn't read the tabloids."

Kinga snorted. "My grandfather is as sharp as a tack—he's sure to have read them. Anyway, you survived and he wasn't particularly rude to you. And I'm sorry that you had to hear about the entire history of the Ryder-White clan. Congratulations on not falling asleep."

"Hopefully those DNA tests come back soon. If they don't, he might blow a gasket," Griff said, his dimples flashing. "And, for the record, I've yet to meet a parent, or grandparent, I couldn't charm."

Kinga patted his shoulder. "Apart from being gorgeous, you are also incredibly modest and self-effacing."

Griff's laugh, sexy and low, rolled over her. "You are very good at keeping my feet on the ground, Kinga."

"It's tough but I'm up to the challenge," Kinga replied, keeping her voice light. She couldn't let him suspect that it was a job she wouldn't mind doing for a long time. The thought made her feel icy cold.

She'd never give a man, *anyone*, that much power over her. No, it was better to be like her parents, uninvolved and unemotional. They weren't blissfully happy but they *were* reasonably content. Reasonably content was all anyone could ask for, right?

Asking for more was looking for heartbreak.

She should end this, sooner rather than later. Maybe Griff would hand her a way to ease out of his life with the minimum of drama. They did, after all, still have to work together.

"Changing the subject… Have you heard from that prick again?" Griff demanded, annoyance tingeing his words.

"Mick?"

Unfortunately, she had. He'd left a voice message, apologizing for going to Viola's and begging for a meeting with Kinga to clear the air. He suggested dinner at his house and the thought made her want to vomit.

Was she imagining the red in Griff's eyes? Deciding not to tell him about the dinner invite, she deflected. "I heard from one of my journalist friends that he's sent out an invitation to a very exclusive cocktail party. My source says he's been teasing a big announcement, but his political ambitions are an open secret."

"When is this cocktail party?"

"Uh, on the second, I think. At one of the restaurants downtown. Very smart, very ritzy. The media is invited, too. My friend says most of them are going only because of the free snacks and an open bar."

"So he's going to get his time in the spotlight?" Griff asked.

"Sounds like it. If the press doesn't make a big

song and dance about his bid, he'll find it harder to break into the news cycle and to get his face before the public." Kinga frowned at him, suspicious. "You aren't planning on gate-crashing his party, are you?"

Griff raised one arrogant eyebrow. "And give him the press coverage he wants? Hell, no. Though I wouldn't mind meeting him in a dark alley and seeing how he likes to be on the receiving end of *my* fist," he added.

Maybe it wasn't politically correct, but there was something lovely about having a strong, protective man in her corner, prepared to stand between her and the world.

But…

But Griff was temporary, someone who wasn't sticking around. She couldn't start relying on him.

Besides, she was a strong and independent woman who could handle herself.

*And don't you dare forget that, Ryder-White.*

Griff turned his head and looked at Kinga's delicate profile, soft and vulnerable and relaxed. This trip to NYC was an unexpected pleasure. After they were finished with work, he planned on taking her to a little restaurant in Brooklyn, a ten-seater Italian joint that served the best shrimp and lemon risotto he'd ever tasted. And amazing tiramisu. Maybe they could get takeout and have another threesome…

The last one, with the cheesecake, had been a bunch of fun.

Griff hoped he'd be able to fly under the radar in

the city and, if he took the normal precautions, ball cap and sunglasses, hopefully nobody would know he was there. He knew Kinga had booked a suite at the hotel but he wondered if that was wise as chambermaids and bellhops were a frequent source of information for the paparazzi.

And if the press found out he was sleeping with Kinga Ryder-White, their lives would be untenable. She was a good girl, Portland's princess, and he was Hollywood's favorite bad boy. It wouldn't be the first or the hundredth time his love life was dissected for the titillation of the public, but he was pretty sure Kinga—or her father or grandfather—would not appreciate the invasion of her privacy.

Nor would her family appreciate the fact that she was mixing business with pleasure...

Kinga was so different from anyone he'd dated before. She was supersmart and very independent, sophisticated but not hard. A little more vulnerable than he was comfortable with. All his previous lovers understood that, by being at his side, there was always the chance their affair would hit the tabloids. For some, the notoriety was an added inducement, hoping they'd be able to leverage the publicity into something bigger and bolder.

Kinga was not like that. She was different, in a hundred ways, all of them pleasurable. Griff looked at her, blonde and beautiful but not in a centerfold pinup type of way, and his heart thumped against his rib cage, while his stomach attempted a backflip.

He'd been in lust before—many times—but no one had ever made his internal organs quiver.

Not that he was in love with Kinga Ryder-White—it was an unrealistic, silly concept, but she affected him in ways no woman ever had. He didn't like it.

Then again, there were a million things he didn't like but couldn't change.

Griff heard the ding of a message landing on his phone. It was a video clip of Sam on the beach, chasing seagulls and whooping like a banshee. Seeing Kinga's curious expression at the noises coming from his phone, he angled his screen and pushed Play again.

"That's Sam, my nephew."

Griff almost looked around to see who had said his words, who was using his voice. Astounded that he'd told her something so incredibly personal, he immediately turned his head to look out the window, unable to meet her eyes.

*"Sian has a child?"*

He'd opened the door, allowed her to walk inside; he couldn't shut her out now. He wanted to but manners dictated that he had to, at the very least, give her a small explanation.

"Yes, but I've helped raise him since he was born. Sian lives on my Kentucky ranch and Sam and I are very close," Griff added, pushing his hand through his hair, wishing he'd kept his mouth shut.

"He's very cute."

"He's my world."

And he was sharing his existence with Kinga.

His stomach dropped, as heavy as an iron bar.

He'd just exposed himself. Worse, he'd exposed his family to a woman he barely knew and wasn't sure he could trust. Not because Kinga was untrustworthy but because he didn't trust anybody, not with information about Sian and Sam. He'd never even brought a woman home to meet his family; the thought had never crossed his mind. It wasn't what he did, who he was.

He and Sian had had their fights because he was so very protective—she'd, on more than one occasion, accused him of smothering her—but it wasn't because he didn't trust or respect her. She was his sister, damn it. The person he shared a womb with; he couldn't *not* look out for her. "He looks like you. How old is he?" Kinga asked. He looked at her and saw more questions in her eyes, including the one she most wanted to know but dare not ask…

*Who was the father of Sian's child?*

He dropped his head to look at the floor, unsure how much to tell her. He quickly tallied up the pros and cons. If he said nothing and she let the information slip about Sam, he might be able to refute her words, to dismiss her claim.

But if he gave her more, and she let all of it slip, the media's interest in Sian would be reignited. And if the world found out Finn was Sam's father, the internet would explode.

And Sian would be hounded… His sister wasn't ready, might never be strong enough, for so much concentrated attention.

It all came down to whether he trusted Kinga or not. And really, how could he? He liked her, her body enthralled him and he enjoyed her quick mind. But realistically, he hadn't spent enough time with her to trust her with his most explosive secrets.

"You don't trust me."

Griff raised his head and looked into her pale, wounded face. "Try not to take it personally. I don't trust anybody. I should never have told you about Sam."

"Why did you?" Kinga quietly asked him, nervous fingers drumming on her thigh.

He jerked a shoulder up. "I'm not sure, actually. It kinda slipped out." Griff looked into her lovely eyes and saw her hurt and disappointment. Dammit. He never meant to make her feel either emotion. How could he explain his fears without insulting her? "I have a lot of trust issues, Kinga."

She nodded. "I'm sure you do. I'm sure growing up in a superficial world with superficial people has scared you, made you wary."

"Not everyone in the industry is shallow and superficial. I've met some lovely people, like Stan and Ava."

"But more people let you down than supported you," Kinga pointed out. He couldn't argue with that. And the person he trusted the most, with his career and with his sister, had done the most damage.

Before he could reply, Kinga spoke again. "And you don't know whether your impulsive confession will backfire on you spectacularly."

Yeah, well. *That.*

"I'm not a groupie, neither am I easily impressed with stardom," Kinga told him, sounding pissy. "I thought you understood that." She pushed a finger into his shoulder. "I went to bed with Griff, the man, not Griff, the star. I don't even like Griff, the star with the stunning voice."

*Ouch.*

But the pain was clean, sweet rather than jagged. And in her eyes, he saw that she spoke the truth. But he needed to hammer home the point.

"If the press found out Sian has a son, the ramifications could be devastating, Kinga," Griff said, his voice as cold as an Arctic storm. He saw her eyebrows lift and knew she thought he was being melodramatic. But he couldn't explain. That level of trust had died with Finn.

"Your secret is safe with me, Griff. I'd never betray you," Kinga stated, and Griff knew that she'd try to keep that promise. That didn't mean she would.

"If it helps relieve your anxiety, I'm not an impulsive person," Kinga explained. "I always have a backup plan, maybe two. I overthink everything and I never, ever make quick decisions. So the chances of something slipping out, as you say, are minimal."

"I know I sound like an asshole, but…" Griff rubbed the back of his neck. Kinga placed a hand on his shoulder and squeezed.

"I get it, Griff, I do. The less I know, the less you'll stress," Kinga nodded. "But…" she added, pulling her bottom lip between pretty teeth, "…given your trust issues and my fear of doing something stupid, maybe this is a good time to have a conversation about us…"

She was going to tell him something he didn't want to hear, like she couldn't see him anymore.

"I can't keep doing this."

Was he a genius or what? Griff cocked his head, silently asking for more of an explanation. Kinga twisted the ring on her middle finger, a colorful concoction of brightly colored stones.

"You've slipped under my skin," she admitted, her frustration obvious.

And he had no problem admitting, to himself, that she was deep under his…

"It normally takes me ages to feel comfortable with somebody, longer if that person is a man. And I've never felt as comfortable with a guy—or anyone since Jas—as I do with you. That scares me because I can see myself falling for you and I don't want to do that. I don't want to risk falling for anyone. I can't risk losing someone I lov—like, again. I can't do it. I don't *want* to do it."

Griff stared at her, unable to believe they were having this conversation thirty thousand feet in the air.

"I'm thinking that we should stop this, Griff, before it runs away with us," Kinga ran her hand through her hair. "We both know it could never work."

Did they know that?

"Explain it to me…"

Kinga's expression was pure who-are-you-kidding? After hesitating, she sighed and lifted her shoulders, allowing them to drop quickly. She lifted her leg off his and withdrew from him, putting as much space as possible between them.

*Shit.*

"You live in Kentucky, and in Nashville." She wrinkled her nose. "In fact, I don't even know what property you call your true home."

He loved his homes in Nashville and Malibu but also loved being on the ranch in Kentucky. He loved spending time in Key Largo... Asking which place was his true home was a good question and one he didn't know the answer to.

"I am a Mainer," she said. "I will always want to live in Portland. My job is there and my family is close by, even if they are occasionally a little odd. You're impulsive and free-spirited, I'm...not. I hate the idea of living my life in a fishbowl and that's where you need to be, in the public eye."

To a point. He'd proved these past two or so years that he could lead a low-key life.

Griff opened his mouth to argue with her and snapped it closed, unable to believe he was about to put forward a case about why they should be together, stay together.

"I have a ball to organize and after that's done, I have other projects that will take up my time. I'm burning the candle at both ends, juggling sleeping with you and trying to stage one of the biggest functions of the decade and my career. My concentration is shot and I'm rapidly heading toward burnout. I can't afford to screw up, Griff. This is a once-in-a-lifetime event for Ryder International. We both should put all our energies toward making the ball a success. You because it will make your comeback easier if you nail your performance, me because, well, I don't want to disappoint myself or my family.

"You've got to admit that there's nothing we can build on, Griff. No common friends, no common city, God, I can't even sing!" Kinga wailed.

Funny, he so didn't care. He forced a smile onto his face. "Yep, that's a deal breaker."

"I'm being serious, Griff."

"I know."

And she was right, Griff reluctantly admitted. There were just a couple weeks—three? four?—before the ball and he needed to get his head in the game and start rehearsing his ass off. He needed his performance to be his best yet. Because he hadn't done this in a while, he was rusty. With Kinga being so busy, too, he'd be lucky to get scraps of her time, and he was far too selfish and demanding to be content with that.

But he knew he was going to regret letting this extraordinary woman leave his life.

He knew that truth like he knew his name. She was the first person who'd ever made him consider more... a relationship, a life together, building a future.

Ridiculously, he wanted her to meet his twin, Sam, his older sister and his brother-in-law. He already knew that Eloise, wise and wonderful, would love Kinga.

But what choice did he have but to agree with her to call this quits? She already knew too much and if they carried on seeing each other, he knew he'd tell her more, possibly everything, and she'd be the keeper of all his secrets. If she betrayed him, she'd not only devastate him but Sian and Sam, too. The stories would dog Sam his entire life. This wasn't just about Griff...

And she wanted out. He'd never been dumped before...

It sucked.

But Kinga was right. They should end this before things turned deeper, more intense. It would be better this way: a relationship always hit roadblocks, dived off cliffs, tore apart souls, eventually.

"So, are we going to go to the hotel, check out the function room and fly back? If that's the case, I might spend an extra few days in the city."

Kinga lowered her lashes and hauled in a deep breath, and Griff watched her cheeks turn pink. "Well, I was thinking we could go our separate ways tomorrow. That is, if you want one more night..."

More than he wanted his heart to keep beating.

Relief crashed over him, hot and sweet. Thank God. And screw the Italian restaurant, he was keeping her in bed for as long as he possibly could. He had memories to make...

He cradled her cheek in the palm of his hand and dropped a gentle kiss on her temple, holding his lips there, breathing her in. This was the start of twenty-four hours of trying to imprint her body, her smell, the wonderfulness of her on his soul. "In case I forget to tell you tomorrow, I have loved every second of being with you."

When he pulled back, he saw the sheen of tears in her eyes. She covered his hand with hers, holding his in place. "If this were another time or place, if we both didn't have so much damn baggage…"

"Yeah. If only…" Griff pulled back, knowing that if he started kissing her, he wouldn't stop. Then again, if this was all the time they had, he was wasting it.

"Does this plane have a bedroom?" he asked, seeing the heat in her eyes.

"It does," Kinga told him, after sucking his bottom lip between her teeth and releasing it with a plop. "But unfortunately, we're descending and will be landing in ten or so minutes."

Griff captured her chin in his hands and gave her a hard kiss, trying to ignore the desire in her eyes. How was he supposed to let her go when she looked at him like that? "Bed first, ballroom later?"

Kinga stroked her finger along his jaw, loving the scratchy feel of his stubble. "It's a deal, O'Hare. And, Griff?"

"Yeah?"

"In case I forget to mention it, I had the best time, too." She smiled, releasing a small, forced laugh. "Thanks for showing me a different way to eat cheesecake."

\* \* \*

Thinking about wearing a black tuxedo, black tie for my performance on the 14th.

Sounds perfect, Kinga replied.

Brief emails and text messages were how she and Griff communicated these days and, over the last three weeks, many days had passed without them touching base at all. She set up the publicity events, he attended them and always managed to steer the conversation back to Ryder International's hundred years in business, their ball and the Ryder Foundation.

Remaining calm, he charmed the interviewers, insisting that he was still exploring his options career-wise and hadn't decided on a clear path.

It wasn't a path she would be walking with him...

Another message popped up on her screen: I'm thinking of dressing the backup singers in bright red sequins with white collars and big, heart brooches.

Knowing he was teasing—because, well, he knew she'd disembowel him if he did that—Kinga responded with a tongue-out emoji and returned her attention to her laptop sitting on the coffee table in front of her, needing to make sense of her master list for the ball, a detailed, massive, color-coded document.

Sitting on the cozy two-seater couch in her office, Kinga felt the familiar burn and reached for the box of antacids on the table next to her. She popped out four, chewed them and prayed for them to work. Her heart was on fire; there was a huge boulder sitting on her chest and a massive, invisible python was wrapped around her ribs.

Her stress-induced indigestion would pass. She just needed the ball to be a success and, after the fourteenth, she would feel like herself again. She was slated to take a two-week holiday, but she'd yet to decide where to go or what to do. Frankly, what she most wanted to do was hole up in her apartment and sleep for a week.

She missed Griff.

No, she missed him *desperately*. Missed his intelligent eyes and rough voice, his agile mind and his truly excellent body. They barely knew each other, had barely scraped the surface of what made each other tick, but Kinga knew he had the potential to be someone special in her life.

Hell, he already was.

The truth was that she was mourning a relationship that was never fully formed, and the love she felt for a man she could never be with. He was the one she wanted at her side, the one she couldn't live without, the puzzle piece she'd been missing.

But she'd sent him away because she was scared… scared to try, scared to love, scared to lose.

But since he wasn't in love with her, what choice did she have?

Kinga looked up as her office door opened and she pulled up a smile as Tinsley walked into her office and dropped into the seat next to her. She placed her hand on Kinga's back, and Kinga tipped her head sideways so it connected with her sister's.

"It's late, sweetie. Let's go home," Tinsley suggested.

Kinga frowned at the darkness beyond her window and glanced at her watch. It was past nine already—where had the time gone? And what had she accomplished? Not that much…

Tinsley leaned forward and picked up the box of antacids, her navy eyes concerned. "This box was full this morning, Kinga."

Yeah, she was pretty sure she had an ulcer but she had no time to get it checked out. After the ball, she would, as she told Tinsley.

"Let's hope it doesn't perforate before then," Tinsley muttered.

It wasn't a cheerful thought and Kinga hoped so, too. That would suck.

"Did you get the invitation to Mick's cocktail party?" Tinsley asked.

Kinga pulled a face. "I did."

She'd finally confessed Mick's actions to Tinsley and her confession had resulted in a few lectures about keeping stuff to herself and being stupidly independent.

"Are you going?" Kinga asked her sister.

"Hell, no!" Tinsley's smile was just this side of evil. "And I'm telling everyone I can think of not to go, either. Mom, Dad and Seth are also encouraging all their friends and connections—and between us, we know everyone—to boycott the function and his mayoral campaign," Tinsley said, looking smug.

"I don't think he's going to have much support. If only we could get the press to boycott him as well."

"It's a story connected to Jas and those will always sell," Kinga told her. She squeezed Tinsley's knee. "But thank you for doing that."

Tinsley smiled before her expression turned concerned. "How are you, Kinga?"

She started to insist that she was fine before admitting she was tired of lying, tired of trying to be strong. This was, after all, her sister. And her best friend. "I'm stressed about the ball and overworked, but mostly I simply miss Griff."

Tinsley didn't look pleased and Kinga couldn't blame her. She wasn't happy that the bad boy of rock and roll had caused such emotional chaos, either.

"It was never anything serious, but it also feels like it was. I'm not sleeping much. I'm often awake at three a.m., bawling my eyes out, missing something I never had. Missing someone who was never mine."

Tinsley thought for a moment before wrapping her arm around Kinga's shoulders. "Would it help you if I reminded you that he's a bad boy rebel, a Peter Pan, someone who'll never grown up? He's done a million stupid things, he's irresponsible and selfish, and if he messes up at the ball, his career will be over, forever."

"But that's the thing, Tins. After our first meeting, I never thought of him in those terms again. He's never been *that* guy, to me. Sometimes I think he's better at *playing* the bad boy, than *being* the bad boy."

"Really?"

Kinga shrugged. "I can't explain why but I know the rebel persona is not who he is, not really." The real Griff was tough but tender, alpha to his core but considerate, too. A little sweet, a little arrogant, flawed and fabulous. A guy who adored his sister, was obviously in love with his nephew, who kept in constant touch with his family.

And she missed him with every breath she took.

Kinga waved her hands in front of her face, trying to dry the tears in her eyes. "Let's talk about something else, anything else. Tell me something to distract me, Tins."

"Okay." Tinsley leaned back against the arm of her chair, folded her arms and lifted one arched eyebrow. "Let's see…the parents are still acting weird and if they ask me one more time why the DNA tests have been delayed, I might lose it. And today I heard that Garrett Kaye will be attending our ball."

Garrett Kaye was the wealthy venture capitalist son of Callum's personal assistant, Emma. Kinga felt a little of her misery recede at this news. They'd only met him a few times over the years and, while fabulous-looking, he was tight-lipped, introverted and frequently abrasive. But he was one of the richest men in the country and his attending the ball would give it another level of cachet. If Garrett Kaye thought the ball worth attending then it had to be something special…

"That's great news."

Tinsley smiled. "He's not bringing a plus-one, so

we'll put him at the same table with the other singles, like Jules. And Sutton Marchant, Cody and others."

Sutton Marchant was a mega-wealthy ex–international trader who'd found fame when his debut novel hit the New York bestseller list. Kinga had met him years ago in London and found him bright, fantastically good-looking and quietly charming. Garrett Kaye probably wouldn't contribute much to the conversation but Sutton and Jules, their best friend and world renowned mixologist, would keep their table entertained when Griff wasn't performing.

Griff…her thoughts always went back to the man who'd upended her world.

# Nine

In Key Largo, Griff lay on his back on a lounger in swim trunks, Sam curled up next to him, fast asleep. It was late afternoon, and his nephew was exhausted after a day on the beach. Griff felt like he could drift off, too.

But he knew that as soon as he closed his eyes, his brain would kick into high gear and sleep would scuttle off like a crab. God, he was tired.

He and his band had been practicing flat out and their performance was practically flawless. They'd worked out the kinks, rearranged the set list, added some songs, dropped others. Knowing they all needed a break—and that if he didn't leave Portland he wouldn't be able to resist rocking up on Kinga's doorstep and begging her to let him in, take him back, make it work—he'd told his crew to take a long weekend and headed down to the Keys.

But Kinga was always with him…

Griff sighed. Even if she wanted him in her life, and as far as he knew she didn't, he still couldn't tell her the truth about his past. And Kinga deserved someone who was all in, someone who trusted and loved her enough to open the closet door and show her all the skeletons inside.

He couldn't do that, not when all the skeletons he'd helped bury weren't his…

To distract himself from thoughts of his brown-eyed pixie, Griff thought about the news sites he'd visited earlier: the news from Portland and the East Coast was the same as it ever was. He read lots of articles reporting on the ball and on his comeback, but there were a few about what was being touted as the party-before-the-ball, Pritchard-the-Prick's event. The press was speculating that he was going to announce his decision to enter politics—like that world needed more scumbags.

He hoped Kinga was okay, that she wasn't being hassled or harassed. God, why had Griff left Portland?

He sighed, lifted his bottle to his lips and sighed again. Suddenly noticing the silence, broken only by waves hitting the beach, gulls and Sam's soft snore, he looked around and found four sets of eyes on him.

"What?" he demanded, placing his empty beer bottle on the table beside him. He wouldn't mind another, but that would mean disturbing Sam, who'd only just nodded off.

Griff looked over the rails of the balcony to the white sands and clear water below and considered going for a run or hitting the state-of-the-art gym downstairs after Sam woke up. But he'd done both already today and was still waiting for a rush of endorphins.

He was starting to believe his happy hormone was called Kinga Ryder-White.

Griff rubbed the skin above his heart in a futile attempt to close the hole that was growing bigger by the day. Crap, he missed her. He missed her smile, her scent, her raspy voice and take-no-shit attitude.

He was grieving the end of something that had never really begun.

"Fool."

"We've been telling you that for years," Sian said, and Griff realized that he'd spoken aloud. Marvelous. And because he'd opened the door, they'd step on in and pepper him with questions...

Three, two, one...

"Why are you grumpy?" Jan demanded.

"You look like the dog ate your homework, dude," Pete commented.

"What's been happening in Portland that's made you so depressed?" Sian asked him. She was doing really well on her new medication. She seemed to be enjoying mothering Sam and she was interacting with the family more than she had in a long time.

Maybe his twin was on her way to stability... Oh,

he couldn't kid himself—she'd have setbacks and episodes for the rest of her life, but if she could remain as upbeat as she currently was, he'd consider that a massive win.

Unlike him, who was feeling anything but positive.

He didn't know where he wanted his career to go but knew he was done, forever, with acting like the irresponsible man-child the world thought he was. He also knew he would never take on a movie role, act in a play, release an album or do a performance unless the project resonated with him.

He wanted to work at his craft and create a legacy people could respect. He wanted to be the type of man who deserved a woman like Kinga, someone she could be proud of...

Yet he knew that no matter where he went or what he did, his past would follow him. It was now a part of his persona, not easily discarded.

He closed his eyes and released another long stream of air.

Eloise, sitting beside him, patted his hand. "I've known you since you were a child, Griff, and I don't think I've ever seen you so blue. Why don't you tell us what's worrying you?"

*Uh, that would be a hard no.*

He was the protector of his family, the one responsible for making the ship sail smoothly. He'd pull himself off the rocks, just as soon as he got his head together. But until then, he'd pretend, as he always did, that nothing was wrong.

"I'm fine, Eloise. Everything is fine."

"Not, it's not!" Sian whisper-shouted, obviously not wanting to wake Sam. But her voice crept up to normal levels as she spoke. "You and I need to talk, twin."

"Nothing to talk about," Griff eyed her, noticing the militant look in her eye. "I *am* fine."

"Bullshit!" Sian replied, leaning forward. She caught his eye and Griff saw she was clear-eyed and determined. Strong…

His heart surged with pride.

"Look, I know that I haven't been well for a long time and I accept I have issues and always will. But the new medication I'm on is helping, a lot. I don't feel as disconnected as I once did. A few years ago, I didn't care whether I lived or died, whether you or Sam or Jan lived or died. I might feel like that again in the future, and I really am going to work hard not to feel like that, but today I feel like myself."

Griff smiled at her. "I'm glad you are feeling stronger, twin. You and Sam are my priority, you know that."

"I do."

Good, conversation over. Time to get another beer—

"But Sam and I aren't the only people in this family who deserve to be happy," Sian told him. She smiled as Jan sat on the arm of her chair, their older sister silently offering Sian her support. "You deserve to be happy, too, Griff."

Griff thought about protesting but didn't have the

energy. Happiness…it was such an intangible emotion. The closest he'd come to the emotion were those few nights he'd spent with Kinga…

Why did everything come back to her?

"I want to set the record straight, Griff," Sian stated, her tone and expression resolute. "I want to tell the world my story, the whole story."

Not happening. Not ever.

Griff looked from Jan to Pete, and neither looked surprised at Sian's announcement. So, this wasn't the first time this issue had been discussed.

"No," Griff declared. "Not a chance in hell."

"I can do it with or without you, Griff."

Her warning shocked him, causing him to rise abruptly. Sam tipped to the side and Griff caught him before he woke up and gently lowered the boy to the cushion. When he was certain Sam was comfortable, Griff walked over to the railing, gratefully snagging the beer Pete held out to him.

"I don't understand why you want to expose yourself, Sian. Why you'd want to undo years and years of hard work," Griff muttered. Years of *his* hard work.

She hit him with a clear-eyed look. "I want to tell the truth, the real truth. I want to set myself, and you, free. I still have a voice, a loud voice, and I can be an advocate for people with mental health issues. But to use that voice, to do some good, I need to be honest. I *must* be honest. And so do you… The world needs to know why you did what you did, that all your crap was to take the focus off me. I needed your help back then, I don't need it as much now. I'm stronger, better, *bolder*. If we tell the truth, the weight will be lifted off both of us. You can reclaim your name—"

"I don't care what the world thinks about me!" Griff told her. Outside this group, and Stan and Ava, he only cared about the thoughts and feelings of one person, just *one*.

He just wanted to tell Kinga, not the entire freakin' world.

"The press will go insane, you will be stalked and hounded." Griff pushed his hand through his hair. "You won't be able to move without being ambushed by a reporter with a camera."

This was such a bad idea. He couldn't believe that Jan and Pete supported this BS.

Sian shrugged. "We've discussed that. The ranch is completely secure and so is this island. I've spoken to my therapist, Griff, and I intend to be very careful about how I wade into this unknown territory. I mostly intend to work via social media, and I will be extremely cautious about any public appearances. Sam, his happiness, safety and security, will always be my top priority. Everything I do will be carefully vetted and screened by my therapist and my security team."

"You have a security team?" he asked, sending Pete a what-the-hell look.

"No, but I will get one," Sian told him, looking earnest. She stood up and walked over to him and placed her hand on his bare forearm. "I want to reclaim my life, Griff. I *need* to reclaim it."

He didn't like it at all. "Okay, I hear you. But

you don't need to explain the past. Just put out a press release saying you have had difficulties and that you intend to be an advocate for people with mental health struggles."

"And be accused of being just another celebrity who won't get her hands or reputation dirty?" Sian scoffed and shook her head. "No, I either do this properly or I don't do it at all."

This was Sian—feisty, determined and difficult to sway once she'd decided on a course of action. Griff pulled his eyes off her stubborn face to look at the trio watching them interact.

"I presume you've had the same argument with her?" he asked.

Jan nodded. "We've covered the same ground, many, many times."

"I'm afraid we have two choices, my dear," Eloise said. "We can either support her and stand by her side, or we can watch her do this on her own. I vote for the first."

Sian started to talk, but Griff held up his hand, asking her to give him a minute. He needed to think. Sian was going to expose his bad boy life as a sham, tell the world why he acted like he did, and after that, there'd be no secrets to keep. He couldn't help feeling excited at having that burden lifted.

It would no longer be his burden.

Maybe it never had been.

Sian was going to do this, with or without him, and he was damned if he wouldn't stand by her side. He'd always thought she was talented, very smart, but today he was so very proud of her strength, in awe of her courage.

Man, he was so very proud to be her brother. Her twin.

And sometime in the future, when the furor died down and his life settled into a new type of normal, maybe he could ask Kinga out for dinner, start afresh, with no secrets between them.

A guy could only hope.

Griff narrowed his eyes, a thought occurring. Maybe, just maybe, he could kill a flock of birds with one supercharged stone...

"Are you sure you want to do this, Sian?"

Sian rolled her eyes before solemnly nodding. "I am very sure, Griff. If I could do it today, I would."

Right, well...

Griff looked into her eyes, so like his own. "If you are certain, if you are irrevocably committed to this path, can I ask you to do something for *me*?"

It was past six and Kinga promised herself an early night, vowed not to work until the early hours of the evening. She was even thinking about leaving her laptop here in her office, to force herself to take a break.

She was still debating whether she'd curse herself for such a radical move when Tinsley flew into Kinga's office, her expression confused.

"News!" Tinsley dramatically announced.

"Good or bad?" Kinga asked her overexcited sister, unable to summon much interest. God, she had to pull herself together. Since she and Griff parted ways, nothing much raised her blood pressure.

"I drove past the restaurant where Pritchard is hosting his cocktail party and not only is there a dearth of guests, but I also can't see any members of the media, either."

"They are probably all inside the restaurant, Tins."

Tinsley sat on the edge of her desk. "They aren't. As I drove past, I saw three reporters leaving the venue, moving fast. I think something else has happened to take the spotlight off Pritchard."

Kinga shrugged, not particularly concerned. Mick was a jerk and she refused to let him affect her life anymore. Jas was gone. Kinga still loved her and she was pretty sure that wherever Jas was, she still loved Kinga, too. It was time to release the guilt… well, as much as she could.

"What could've happened to drag their attention away from Pritchard? O'Hare is still out of town, so it can't be him," Tinsley stated, frowning. "It's got to be a big story."

Her sister was curious, and Kinga knew she wouldn't leave until she knew what was happening and where. Tinsley hated being out of the loop.

"Contact your sources," Kinga told Tinsley, pulling her phone out of her bag. Scrolling through her contacts list, she called one reporter, didn't receive an answer, and called another. Judging by Tinsley's face, she wasn't getting much joy, either.

Frustrated, Kinga punched out a text message, staring at her phone as she waited for a reply. A minute later her phoned vibrated, indicating an incoming message from one of her favorite journalists.

Sian O'Hare is giving a press conference at the Portland Harbor Hotel. Heady stuff. The place is packed, every reporter ever born is here. Guess that's the O'Hare pulling power.

WTH? Kinga replied. Is Griff there?

Griff and Stan and Ava. Wow. He did a great job snowing us.

What on earth did that mean? Kinga read out the messages to Tinsley, who looked equally astonished. Kinga tried to imagine why Griff would call a press meeting without telling her and felt her stomach twist into a tangled knot. What if he was pulling out of the concert? What if he was announcing his retirement, telling the world he was going on a retreat to find inner peace?

Kinga verbalized her fears to Tinsley, who frowned. "If that's the case, then I'll personally track him down and drag him back to Portland by his hair. Let's go find out what he's up to, Kingaroo."

Kinga followed Tinsley to her car, her stomach burning and her head pounding.

*I won't let you down.*

Kinga remembered his words and his determined eyes and her shoulders dropped and her tension eased away. She didn't know what this was about, but Griff wouldn't let her down. He'd said he'd be there for her and he would be.

"He won't disappoint me, Tins," Kinga told Tinsley as she negotiated her way through the evening traffic to the Portland Harbor Hotel.

"Okay," Tinsley said, sounding doubtful, slipping her car between a delivery van and an SUV.

"It'll be okay, I promise."

Tinsley tossed her a quick look and then a smile. "Of course it will, because my sister—cautious, analytical and very wary of making mistakes—would never fall in love with a man who would let her down."

Kinga considered Tinsley's words, and when they sank in, she smiled. Damn straight. He might not love her and he couldn't give her the life she wanted—to shelter in his arms, to make babies with him, to live and love and laugh with him—but she was too smart to fall in love with someone who was flaky and foolish.

No, whatever this was about, Griff would still perform at their ball the following weekend.

Tinsley pulled up next to the corner entrance of the redbrick hotel, telling her that she'd find a parking space and meet her as soon as she could. Kinga nodded, exited the vehicle, and raised her hand in apology to the driver in the car behind them. Adjusting her bag on her shoulder, she entered the lobby of the lovely hotel and walked up to the front desk, asking where the press conference was being held.

Ten minutes later, she slipped into the biggest of

their conference rooms, her eyebrows lifting at the number of people in the room. A feminine voice was talking about being an ambassador for mental health and the journalists were entranced by whatever she was saying, heads lifting and falling as pens flew across notepads. Unable to see Griff, his sister or anyone else, Kinga edged down the wall until she was at the front of the packed crowd. Standing behind a diminutive journalist with a fearsome reputation, she looked at the table in front of her, her breath catching as her eyes fell on her favorite X-rated fantasy man who was wearing a...

Kinga squinted, unable to believe her eyes. Was Griff wearing a suit? Yep, dark gray, with a white shirt and patterned tie in greens and blues. He was also clean-shaven, his hair was neatly brushed, and he looked like a Wall Street trader, someone who frequented Ryder's Bar in Manhattan.

She far preferred him in ripped jeans and a tight T-shirt.

Her eyes danced over the rest of the table. Ava Maxwell sat between Griff and her husband, looking as she always did, indescribably lovely. Stan wore his usual black and his expression was both bored and forbidding. Griff's arm rested on the back of his twin's chair, a clear signal that she was under his protection.

Sian was the feminine version of her brother, with darker hair, green eyes and the same sexy mouth. She was tall and thin, and while her mouth was pulled up into a practiced smile, her eyes looked tired.

Griff kept his eyes on her profile and, as if hearing her thoughts, leaned forward to speak into his microphone. "I think that's enough for today, folks." When the room responded with collective disappointment, he shook his head, his expression hardening. "You guys have enough for several articles and any other questions can be directed to our publicist…"

They had a publicist? Since when? And why didn't she know about it?

Griff cleared his throat and the room quieted down. "I would like to remind you about my upcoming concert at the Ryder International ball. I would be grateful if you could mention the ball, that all the money raised through this project will go to the Ryder Foundation and that donations are always welcome."

Without missing a beat, Griff looked straight at her, his smile going from practiced to personal. He winked at her and her insides liquefied.

God, she loved this man. She didn't know what was happening or what bombshells he'd just dropped, but, in front of a dozen cameras, he'd given the ball some truly excellent press.

Bonus points for the bad boy—he'd denied Mick his spot in the sun by calling this press conference at the same time Mick wanted the press at his function.

Griff made some concluding remarks and, all around her, the press started to exit the room. She stayed where she was, watching as Griff, his sister and two of the biggest faces in the celebrity land walked in the opposite direction to a door guarded by two black-suited bodyguards.

Kinga scrubbed her hands over her face, still in the dark. She'd discover the reason for this get-together shortly. Hell, she just had to step outside and anyone would tell her, but for now, she was content to stay where she was. She needed a minute to get her bearings.

She'd been right to trust Griff. He hadn't let her down and wouldn't. He'd be behind the microphone at the ball and as soon as his performance ended, he'd be completely out of her life.

Her heart, struck by an invisible but heavy hammer, shattered anew at the realization. Fighting the urge to drop to her knees, she sucked in a couple of breaths, terrified she was heading toward a panic attack. Oh, God, she'd forgotten how painful it was to love and lose someone and she most definitely didn't need the reminder.

Needing to find Tinsley, Kinga blinked back tears. She was about to follow the last of the stragglers out of the room when she saw one of the beefy security guards approaching her, his expression impassive.

"Ms. Ryder-White?"

"Yes?"

"Mr. O'Hare would like to see you. He's asked me to escort you to his executive suite."

"Okay, thanks. Just give me a minute, I need to tell my sister I've been delayed."

Kinga banged out the text message, shoved her phone in her bag and nodded to the man-in-black.

Kinga's breath evened out and her heart settled. She knew Griff would be leaving her life after the ball, but that wasn't tonight. As long as the broad-shouldered man was leading her to Griff, she'd follow him anywhere. O'Hare was, after all, her personal pot of gold at the end of the rainbow.

The security guard knocked on the door to the suite and it opened a few seconds later. Had Griff been waiting for her? Was he as anxious to see her as she was to see him?

Griff gestured her to enter and nodded to the guard standing behind her. "Thanks, Reynolds. Appreciate your help."

Griff closed the door behind the guard and Kinga's eyes drifted over him. He'd shed his suit jacket and his tie was pulled from his open collar. His hair was now ruffled, as if he'd shoved his hands through it. Frankly, he looked exhausted.

Kinga couldn't help lifting her hand to his cheek, feeling the beginnings of his fast-growing beard. "Are you okay? You look shattered."

"I am tired… That was the hardest thing I've ever done," Griff told her. Placing a hand on her lower back, he guided her into the exquisitely decorated sitting room and suggested she take a seat. "Do you want a drink?"

"No, but you look like you need one," Kinga said, sitting down on the edge of a gray couch. Placing her forearms on her knees, she watched as Griff, obviously distracted, poured himself a shot of whiskey and tossed it back. He then poured another two shots into heavy tumblers and walked back across the room to her, handing her a drink she'd told him she didn't want. Kinga thanked him, placed the drink on the glass coffee table and softly suggested that he sit down.

Griff shook his head and stood behind the chair opposite her, his forearms—sleeves of his shirt rolled up—resting on the top of the chair. Instead of explaining why he'd requested her to come up to his room, he just stared at her, his eyes troubled and his expression brooding.

Unable to contain her curiosity, Kinga spoke. "I have no idea what's going on, why the press pool looks like you just handed them the moon."

"I didn't, Sian did," Griff replied, his voice raspy. His voice always took on that growly quality when he was tired or feeling stressed or emotional. Kinga cocked her head, waiting for him to speak.

He sipped at his whiskey and frowned at her. "It's a long, complicated story."

She didn't have enough patience for long and complicated. "Give me the highlights."

Griff nodded. "Uh...so, in our early to midtwenties we were flying high. If anything, Sian was flying faster and higher than me—she was always the more talented twin." He said those words without any rancor or jealousy. Instead, his voice held a healthy dose of pride.

"You're a pretty talented guy, O'Hare," Kinga pointed out.

He shrugged. "But Sian was next-level good. She was exploring more facets of her talent and people were starting to notice. She was frequently compared to some of the greats, Garland and Hepburn, and was widely considered, by the industry heavyweights, to be a once-in-a-generation performer."

Okay, she hadn't known that.

"Long story short, Sian had always struggled with anxiety and depression, but a few years back she started to behave erratically and, because the press paid so much attention to her, they quickly picked up that something was amiss. They hounded her and the rumors started flying about her using drugs." Griff's frown deepened. "It was, after all, the most logical conclusion."

"But she wasn't," Kinga softly interjected.

"No, she was diagnosed with a mild form of schizophrenia," he said, staring at the glass in his hand. "Her interest in performing declined and she became a bit of a recluse. Her psychiatrist recommended she retreat from the limelight permanently and try to live a life as calm and normal as possible."

"Pretty impossible when you are one of the world's hottest and most recognizable stars," Kinga commented.

"The burning question on everyone's lips—the press, our friends and our colleagues—was why a talented performer at the height of her career would bail? The media interest in her...well, exploded. Finn, our manager, and I both knew we had to do something to change that."

Oh, God, she thought she knew what he was about to say, but because she could be wrong, she waited for him to continue.

"Stan and I have been friends since we were teenagers and he suggested that I start behaving like a spoiled, selfish asshole to pull the attention off Sian."

*Ding! Ding! Ding!* All at once, everything fell into place and Kinga knew her instincts were spot-on.

Griff looked at her, a puzzled expression on his face. "You don't seem surprised."

"I'm not," Kinga told him, picking up her glass and taking a small sip. "For a while now, I've felt that you were playing a role, that you're not who the press portrays you to be."

Griff looked astounded at her almost casual comment. Kinga hid her smile behind her glass and gestured for him to continue. "Carry on with the highlight reel, O'Hare," she told him.

"Finn told me he'd take care of Sian, that he'd keep an eye on her while I went on a tear. We set up a worldwide tour and I caused chaos," Griff reluctantly admitted. "The press attention shifted off Sian and onto me. I behaved like a jerk, but it worked, they bought it."

"And Sian was allowed to fade from view."

Griff stood up and jammed his hands in the pockets of his pants. "Essentially. But Sian is tired of being in the shadows and she wants to help fight the stigma around mental illness. She called the press conference to talk about her diagnosis and explain that I acted like a jerk to protect her. It was her truth to reveal."

"I'm with you so far, but I still don't understand how Stan and Ava fit into this picture."

"The story of Ava and me having an affair was bullshit, and it was a way to give a persistent reporter a scoop."

"So you didn't have a thing with her?"

"Of course, I didn't!" Griff snapped, looking affronted. Then his expression changed to resignation. "Look, all that happened between us was what everyone saw in that club. Sian was pregnant and she'd been spotted, somewhere, I can't remember where, and some intrepid reporter was going to run a story about the baby and her depression. We needed something big and bold to minimize that news, so Ava suggested we fake a hookup. I was reluctant, but Stan agreed with Ava. He's always been super protective of Sian—she's like a little sister to him. We set it up immediately and it worked. The news spread like wildfire."

Kinga couldn't resist asking her next question. "So, what was it like kissing the world's most beautiful woman?"

Griff glared at her. "Stan told me that if my hand landed anywhere other than her back and if my tongue passed her lips, he'd castrate me. I believed him." He shrugged. "Honestly, it was awkward and...*wrong*. Thank God we are both decent actors, because there wasn't a flicker of chemistry between us."

She heard his unspoken words…not like the fire-nado that sprang up between them.

But Kinga couldn't be distracted by the heat in his eyes, the quirk of his sexy lips. There was still so much ground to cover. "Okay, your make-out session with Ava was a scam, but why were they at the press conference? They didn't need to be, not really."

Griff flushed and Kinga thought it was the first time she'd seen him flustered. "Ah, that was for you, actually."

"Me?" What on earth was he talking about? She had nothing to do with his past or their press conference.

"I was reasonably sure the press would drop everything, including Pritchard's cocktail party, to attend Sian's press conference. But I wanted to be certain they would. Because Stan and Ava are seldom in the public eye and never engage with the press, I *knew* every reporter with a heartbeat would attend the press conference if they were there."

Kinga placed her hand on her heart as it flung itself against her rib cage. He'd asked his friends to change a habit of the past few years to deny Mick the publicity he so desperately wanted…and it was all for her. How…sweet. A little Machiavellian but very sweet.

"I don't know what to say," Kinga whispered.

Griff's face hardened and she knew his anger was directed at Mick and not at her. "Friends don't act as he did, and I was happy to put a metaphorical foot on his throat. Besides, Stan is working on a new album and Ava punted her climate change foundation, so they were happy to be there."

"No, they weren't," Kinga countered.

"No, they weren't, but I asked, and they stepped up to the plate. It's what friends do," Griff said on a soft smile.

Yeah, it was what friends did. And by arranging this press conference to coincide with Mick's opening night, Griff had sent him, and her, the message that nobody messed with the people he cared about. And he did care about her, she knew that.

But there was a universe between friendship and love.

"Thank you," Kinga said, her chest and throat tight.

"There's something else you need to know, something media-land doesn't know. It might come out later, or not, but I want to tell you. You'll be the only person who knows, outside of my family and Stan and Ava."

God, he sounded so serious. What on earth could top what he'd already told her? And why was he confiding his secrets to her?

"We can't go forward until everything is in the open," Griff stated, his eyes on hers.

Did he want to go forward? What did that mean?

Kinga clasped her hands together and waited, holding her breath.

"I told you that I left Sian under the care of our manager, Finn. Well, he cared for Sian a little too much. Sam is his biological child."

Holy hell...*what*?

"I was furious. I've always believed that she was in a terrible place, mentally, and that he took advantage of her. Sian says it wasn't like that, that she never felt bullied or coerced." Griff said, his voice saturated with pain and anger. "I was incandescently angry, still am to an extent because she was vulnerable."

He rubbed his palm up and down his jaw. "Anyway...when she was diagnosed, I gained power of attorney over Sian's financial affairs and I fired him the moment I heard. He was on his way to meet with me when he wrapped his car around a tree."

Oh, Griff.

"I was there when Sam was born. Sian suffered from terrible postpartum psychosis and I did all the heavy lifting with Sam, the midnight feedings and the diaper changes. I heard his first word, watched him take his first step. He's Sian's, but in some ways he's also mine. He'll always be a big part of my life."

His love for his nephew radiated from every pore. Seeing his tenderness and unembarrassed adoration for Sam made Kinga fall in love with Griff a little more. If that was even possible.

"From that moment on, I resolved never to trust another person outside of my family and Stan and Ava," Griff said, hoarse with emotion. "Then you came along..."

Kinga stood up slowly, feeling unsteady on her feet. "You trust me?"

Griff's intense eyes didn't leave hers as he slowly nodded. "Trust you implicitly, love you more."

For a moment Kinga thought she'd heard him say he loved her. *Wait!* Did he say he loved her?

"What...what did you say?" she asked, her tone polite.

Griff scrubbed his hands over his face. "I'm in love with you. I know that's not what you want to hear, but I didn't want you to leave my life without you knowing how I feel." He looked a little lost and confused. "I've never felt this way about anyone before, so, yeah, I thought you should know."

Kinga plopped back down on the couch, her legs wobbly and her heart climbing up into her throat. She couldn't believe what she was hearing, couldn't fathom the idea that all her biggest wishes and dreams were within reach.

"Wow...um, that wasn't what I expected," Kinga managed to push the words out.

"I know. It wasn't what I planned, either. I was going to do a comeback concert, release a new album, go on a tour. Maybe pick up a small film role to ease my way back into acting," Griff explained. "Then you dropped into my life and all I can think about is putting my ring on your finger, keeping you in bed for a month, making babies with you."

He looked uncertain and completely out of his depth. "I don't suppose there's a chance you might be interested in any of those?"

Feeling off-balance and knowing she couldn't walk to him on sky-high heels without falling flat on her face, Kinga bent to the side and slowly removed one heel, then the other. Standing up, she carefully circumvented the coffee table, then the chair to stand in front of him. She placed her hands on his chest and, almost instantly, her wobbly world steadied. She felt strength, and love, and happiness flow through her. From him to her and back again.

"No, I wouldn't be interested in one of those," she slowly told him, lifting her mouth to his. She caught the flash of disappointment in his eyes and, not wanting to cause him a moment of pain, hastily added, "I'm interested in all of it."

Shock flashed in Griff's eyes. "What?"

Kinga's laugh was a little tremulous. "You love me, right?"

"Right." His emphatic nod accompanied the word.

"And I love you. You are my…well, you're everything important. You are where I can lay down my insecurities and my fears, my flaws and my failures." Kinga watched as his eyes softened with joy, felt his fingertips digging into her hips. A smile returned to his sexy mouth, and she continued, "You are good sex and quick quips, your arms are where I feel safest and your heart is as big as the sun." The words fell from her lips, a jumble of the good and the glorious. "Oh, I'm making a mess of this! But believe me when I tell you that I love you. Deeply, madly…"

She pulled a face. "And deeply and madly is not what I do, generally."

Griff's hand on her back pulled her to him so

that her breasts pushed into his chest and his erection lay hard against her stomach. "I've missed you so much, sweetheart."

Kinga brushed her lips across his, her mouth curving into a smile. "I've missed you, too." His thumb swiped her bottom lip and Kinga watched, mesmerized, as desire jumped in his eyes.

"What are you thinking, O'Hare?" she asked, as she slowly pulled his shirt out from the back of his pants.

He cupped her ass and squeezed. "That you are the best thing that ever happened to me, that I can't wait for the rest of our lives and that your clothes would look much better on my bedroom floor."

"Shall we test that theory?" Kinga asked him, her hand sliding up his spine.

"Oh, we very much shall…" Griff promised her, scooping her up and holding her against his chest. "But I warn you, it might take a lifetime of experimentation to reach a conclusion."

Kinga sighed, kissed his neck and smiled. She loved and was in love…

Life didn't get much better than this.

* * * * *

*Don't miss the next book in the
Dynasties: DNA Dilemma series!*

Wrong Brother, Right Kiss

*The DNA test results still haven't arrived,
and more changes are coming to the blue-blooded
Ryder-Whites. After one hot New Years' kiss,
Tinsley's attraction to her ex-brother-in-law
proves irresistible...and inconvenient. Did she
marry the wrong brother all those years ago?*

# WE HOPE YOU ENJOYED
## THIS BOOK FROM

### ⬦ HARLEQUIN
# DESIRE

*Luxury, scandal, desire—welcome to
the lives of the American elite.*

Be transported to the worlds of oil barons, family dynasties,
moguls and celebrities. Get ready for juicy plot twists,
delicious sensuality and intriguing scandal.

## 6 NEW BOOKS AVAILABLE EVERY MONTH!

## #2863 WHAT HAPPENS ON VACATION...

*Westmoreland Legacy: The Outlaws* • by Brenda Jackson

Alaskan senator Jessup Outlaw needs an escape...and he finds just the right one on his Napa Valley vacation: actress Paige Novak. What starts as a fling soon gets serious, but a familiar face from Paige's past may ruin everything...

## #2864 THE RANCHER'S RECKONING

*Texas Cattleman's Club: Fathers and Sons* • by Joanne Rock

Pursuing the story of a lifetime, reporter Sierra Morgan reunites a lost baby with his father, rancher Colt Black. He's claiming his heir but needs Sierra's help as a live-in nanny. Will this temporary arrangement withstand the sparks and secrets between them?

## #2865 WRONG BROTHER, RIGHT KISS

*Dynasties: DNA Dilemma* • by Joss Wood

As his brother's ex-wife, Tinsley Ryder-White is off-limits to Cody Gallant. Until one unexpected night of passion after a New Year's kiss leaves them reeling...and keeping their distance until forced to work together. Can they ignore the attraction that threatens their careers and hearts?

## #2866 THE ONE FROM THE WEDDING

*Destination Wedding* • by Katherine Garbera

Jewelry designer Danni Eldridge didn't expect to see Leo Bisset at this destination-wedding weekend. The CEO once undermined her work; now she'll take him down a peg. But one hot night changes everything—until they realize they're competing for the same lucrative business contract.

## #2867 PLAYING BY THE MARRIAGE RULES

by Fiona Brand

To secure his inheritance, oil heir Damon Wyatt needs to marry by midnight. But when his convenient bride never arrives, he's forced to cut a marriage deal with wedding planner Jenna Beaumont, his ex. Will this fake marriage resurrect real attraction?

## #2868 OUT OF THE FRIEND ZONE

*LA Women* • by Sheri WhiteFeather

Reconnecting at a high school reunion, screenwriter Bailey Mitchell and tech giant Wade Butler can't believe how far they've come and how much they've missed one another. Soon they begin a passionate romance, one that might be derailed by a long-held secret...

SPECIAL EXCERPT FROM

**⟨H⟩HARLEQUIN**

# DESIRE

*After the loss of his brother, rancher Nick Hartmann is
suddenly the guardian of his niece. Enter Rose Kelly—
the new tutor. Sparks fly, but with his ranch at stake and
the secrets she's keeping, there's a lot at risk for both...*

*Read on for a sneak peek at*
Montana Legacy
*by Katie Frey.*

The ranch was more than a birthright—it was the thing that
made him a Hartmann. His dad made him promise. Maybe
Nick couldn't voice why that promise was important to him.
Why he cared. His brothers shrugged the responsibility so
easily, but he was shackled by it. His legacy couldn't be
losing the thing that had made him. No. He couldn't fail at
this. Not even to be with her, the mermaid incarnate.

She smiled her odd half smile and splashed some water
at him again. "I don't think you even know all you want,
cowboy." She bit her lip, drawing his attention instantly to
the one thing he'd wanted since meeting her at the airport.
He followed her in a second lap of the pool, catching up to
her in the deep end.

"So your brother married your prom date?" She widened
her eyes as she issued her question.

"It was a long time ago." He cleared his throat. Maybe
Ben was right and he needed to open up a bit.

"Yes, you're practically ancient, aren't you?" She swatted
a bit of water in his direction, which he managed to sidestep.

"Careful, Oxford." He smiled, unable to help himself. It felt good to smile, even more so when faced with the crushing sadness he'd been shouldering for the past three weeks.

"Can you not call me that?" She paused. "My sister went to Oxford. And I don't want to think about her right now."

Her bottom lip jutted forward and quivered. It provoked a response he was unprepared for, and he sealed her concern with a kiss so thorough it rocked him.

Everything he wanted to say he said with the kiss. *I'm sorry. I want you. I'm hurting. Let's forget this.* Her body, hot against his, was a welcome heat to balance the chill of the pool. It was soft and deliciously curved. The perfect answer to his desperate question.

His tongue parried hers and she opened to him with an earnestness that rocked him. A soft mew of submission and he lifted her legs around his, arousal pressed plainly against her. She wrapped her legs around him, the thin skin of the bathing suit a poor barrier, and bit gently at his lip.

"I'm sorry," he started.

"Let's not be sorry, not now." Gone was the sorrow. Instead, she looked at him with a burning fire that he matched with his own.

\

*Don't miss what happens next in*
Montana Legacy
*by Katie Frey.*

*Available April 2022 wherever*
*Harlequin Desire books and ebooks are sold.*

Harlequin.com

# Get 4 FREE REWARDS!

**We'll send you 2 FREE Books <u>plus</u> 2 FREE Mystery Gifts.**

**FREE** Value Over **$20**

Both the **Harlequin® Desire** and **Harlequin Presents®** series feature compelling novels filled with passion, sensuality and intriguing scandals.

---

**YES!** Please send me 2 FREE novels from the Harlequin Desire or Harlequin Presents series and my 2 FREE gifts (gifts are worth about $10 retail). After receiving them, if I don't wish to receive any more books, I can return the shipping statement marked "cancel." If I don't cancel, I will receive 6 brand-new Harlequin Presents Larger-Print books every month and be billed just $5.80 each in the U.S. or $5.99 each in Canada, a savings of at least 11% off the cover price or 6 Harlequin Desire books every month and be billed just $4.55 each in the U.S. or $5.24 each in Canada, a savings of at least 13% off the cover price. It's quite a bargain! Shipping and handling is just 50¢ per book in the U.S. and $1.25 per book in Canada.* I understand that accepting the 2 free books and gifts places me under no obligation to buy anything. I can always return a shipment and cancel at any time. The free books and gifts are mine to keep no matter what I decide.

Choose one: ☐ **Harlequin Desire**
(225/326 HDN GNND)

☐ **Harlequin Presents Larger-Print**
(176/376 HDN GNWY)

Name (please print)

Address _____ Apt. #

City _____ State/Province _____ Zip/Postal Code

**Email:** Please check this box ☐ if you would like to receive newsletters and promotional emails from Harlequin Enterprises ULC and its affiliates. You can unsubscribe anytime.

> Mail to the **Harlequin Reader Service:**
> **IN U.S.A.:** P.O. Box 1341, Buffalo, NY 14240-8531
> **IN CANADA:** P.O. Box 603, Fort Erie, Ontario L2A 5X3
>
> **Want to try 2 free books from another series!** Call 1-800-873-8635 or visit www.ReaderService.com.

*Terms and prices subject to change without notice. Prices do not include sales taxes, which will be charged (if applicable) based on your state or country of residence. Canadian residents will be charged applicable taxes. Offer not valid in Quebec. This offer is limited to one order per household. Books received may not be as shown. Not valid for current subscribers to the Harlequin Presents or Harlequin Desire series. All orders subject to approval. Credit or debit balances in a customer's account(s) may be offset by any other outstanding balance owed by or to the customer. Please allow 4 to 6 weeks for delivery. Offer available while quantities last.

**Your Privacy**—Your information is being collected by Harlequin Enterprises ULC, operating as Harlequin Reader Service. For a complete summary of the information we collect, how we use this information and to whom it is disclosed, please visit our privacy notice located at corporate.harlequin.com/privacy-notice. From time to time we may also exchange your personal information with reputable third parties. If you wish to opt out of this sharing of your personal information, please visit readerservice.com/consumerschoice or call 1-800-873-8635. **Notice to California Residents**—Under California law, you have specific rights to control and access your data. For more information on these rights and how to exercise them, visit corporate.harlequin.com/california-privacy.

HDHP22

# *Love Harlequin romance?*

## DISCOVER.

Be the first to find out about promotions, news and exclusive content!

Facebook.com/HarlequinBooks

Twitter.com/HarlequinBooks

Instagram.com/HarlequinBooks

Pinterest.com/HarlequinBooks

YouTube.com/HarlequinBooks

ReaderService.com

## EXPLORE.

Sign up for the Harlequin e-newsletter and download a free book from any series at
**TryHarlequin.com**

## CONNECT.

Join our Harlequin community to share your thoughts and connect with other romance readers!
**Facebook.com/groups/HarlequinConnection**